WHAT YOU SEE IN THE DARK

Also by Manuel Muñoz

The Faith Healer of Olive Avenue

Zigzagger

WHAT YOU SEE IN THE DARK

A NOVEL BY

MANUEL MUÑOZ

Algonquin Books of Chapel Hill   2011

Published by
ALGONQUIN BOOKS OF CHAPEL HILL
Post Office Box 2225
Chapel Hill, North Carolina 27515-2225

a division of
Workman Publishing
225 Varick Street
New York, New York 10014

A small portion of this novel appeared, in slightly different form, as "Sweet Talk" in *Review: Literature and Arts of the Americas.*

"Last Seen" from *Fate* by Ai. Copyright © 1991 by Ai. Used by permission of W. W. Norton & Company, Inc.

This is a work of fiction. While, as in all fiction, the literary perceptions and insights are based on experience, all names, characters, places, and incidents either are products of the author's imagination or are used fictitiously.

Library of Congress Cataloging-in-Publication Data
Muñoz, Manuel, [date]
What you see in the dark : a novel / by Manuel Muñoz. — 1st ed.
p. cm.
ISBN 978-1-56512-533-9
1. Couples — Fiction.   2. Motion pictures — Production and direction — Fiction.   3. Bakersfield (Calif.) — Fiction.
4. California — History — 1850–1950 — Fiction.   I. Title.
PS3613.U69W47 2011
813'.6 — dc22   2010038452

10 9 8 7 6 5 4 3 2 1
First Edition

For Stuart Bernstein

If the thirst for love
is not the thirst for death, what is it?—

—Ai, "Last Seen"

WHAT YOU SEE IN THE DARK

Part One

One

If you had been across the street, pretending to investigate the local summer roses outside Holliday's Flower Shop, you could have seen them through the café's plate glass, the two sitting in a booth by the window, eating lunch. You could have seen them even if you had been inside the shop, peering from behind the window display of native Bakersfield succulents, wide-faced California sunflowers, blue flax in hanging pots. The two of them sat in full view of everyone passing by, minding their own business. Their mouths moved alternately in long, drawn-out soliloquies, or sometimes they paused and deliberated, as if they had to choose their words carefully, grinning if they spoke at the same time. The girl was eating a thin sandwich and taking short sips from a thick glass of cola. The man ate with a knife and fork, his elbows up in a sawing motion, his eyes sometimes looking down to concentrate.

He was the most handsome man in town for sure, and his mother owned a little motel out on the highway. He always seemed to be wearing only brand-new shirts: no one could keep shirts that color, that softness, time after time, hanging them to dry stiff on a backyard line.

He would be a good man to marry.

They were eating in the café located on one of the choice corners on a better stretch of Union Avenue, the café that still had the plate-glass windows all the way down to the sidewalk, one of the few places that still did after the '52 earthquake. You could see the entire booth through those windows: the table, the red vinyl, their dishes, the waitress's white shoes when she came by to check on them, how the girl crossed her feet and rocked them nervously. She was not dressed as crisply as he was. Even if her clothes looked clean and pressed, you could tell right off that the day she began wearing nice things around town was the day the two of them had done more than talk and have lunch. His mother, whom everybody knew, had worked at the café since before the earthquake, and the waitresses who served him at any of the shifts—breakfast, lunch, dinner, or late-night coffee and cherry pie—had all known him as a boy, so it was hard to tell if their attentions to him were motherly or something more flirtatious.

And yet the one to grab his attention was that skinny brown girl who lived above the bowling alley. Always on foot, always staring into the windows of the record shop, of the TG&Y, of the furniture store, of the Rexall, even of the shoe store where you worked, as if she hadn't set up the displays herself. A very plain girl, not too tall, with slender hips, and hair as dark as her mother's. Her mother had worked at the café, too—with his mother, in fact—almost eight or nine years ago. No doubt his mother remembered.

You could see that girl walking to work at the shoe store, back and forth, going to her apartment during the lunch hour, then home again by the end of the day, no matter what the Valley weather brought: summer heat, fall rains, the terrible winter fog. Even in late November and December, when the sun had gone down by near five o'clock and the streets fell dark, she would walk home alone after the store closed. And that's how it should have stayed, a plain girl like that all alone.

But now this: a thin sandwich and Dan Watson, who was surely going to pay for it, then the waitress coming round with the dessert menu, the girl glancing at the clock, Dan urging her to choose something, then clearly instructing the waitress to hurry back. The waitress indulges him, of course, he being who he is, and comes back with two small silver dishes of vanilla ice cream. He leans over and spoons a small scoop of her ice cream into the cola glass. There is still a lot of soda left, the way she has been sipping it, savoring it. He points for her to take a taste and she does so warily, as if she's never tasted anything like it before. But you have to believe she never has, once that look crosses her face, an amused arch of her eyebrows and a nod of approval.

How people change when they get a taste of the good life! When suddenly the dollar bills in your hand can go for things you want instead of need. A fork-and-knife meal at the café; scarves and pearl chokers; pendants and brooches; jewelry boxes with ballerinas springing to attention; that lovely sound of pushing rings and earrings and bracelets against each other while you're searching. Flowers from Holliday's like the good husbands do: tulips and Easter lilies from Los Angeles in the springtime, a wrist corsage for attending a wedding. A car trip over to the coast, to Morro Bay and the enormous, beautiful rock basking just off the shoreline. A day in Hollywood, the exhilaration of knowing movie stars breathe in the very same sunshine. Silk blouses brought home in delicate paper; dresses that require dry cleaning; lingerie so elegant it refuses to be scandalous.

Is that the life she knows she has ahead of her, the way she is sitting there, her feet rocking nervously after nearly a whole hour? Does she know how every young woman in town wants exactly this? Does she know that people turn their heads to watch them leave the café, to watch him open the door of his Ford truck for her? Does she know people discuss what they've seen, what his mother must think?

Summer carries on, the heat still scorching into September. Harvest time has arrived in Bakersfield and more people have come into town looking for work, whole caravans sometimes. Faces are not as familiar as before, not at the supermarkets, not on the downtown streets. Bakersfield is the open door to the southern part of the state, and the workers come pouring through. So many people have arrived that it becomes difficult to find parking spots, to buy fresh meat, even to get a bench at the Jolly Kone hamburger stand. But this will be short lived— by the end of October, after much of the late-summer crop has been brought in from the fields, the town will go back to normal. The strangers will leave, counting their money, and Bakersfield will wait for those first few weeks of November when the sky goes gray and the fog rolls in over the coastal range and lingers for months on end.

In all the commotion of the harvest boom, most people don't notice that the girl is no longer walking the streets to work. At the lunch hour, she's nowhere to be seen over near Chester Avenue, where her apartment is. But at the shoe store, she's there sure enough, dutifully stepping from the back storage room when Mr. Carson snaps his fingers and tells her the sizes he needs. She never says a word unless a Spanish-speaking customer comes in: this is why she was hired. Mr. Carson cannot refuse the potential business from these customers and leaves the girl to tend to them, stepping away and occupying himself with other business. The girl points to several shoes—she never used to do that!—and smiles boldly at the Spanish-speaking customers, bringing out boxes and boxes for inspection.

Enough word has gotten around town about her eye for beautiful shoes, for high heels that don't necessarily strain the arches, for knowing a budget without having to ask. She moves with confidence and assurance, even if she is not allowed to ring up the sales on her own. She stands nearby to translate, and you handle the money: you, the girl who should be trusted, the kind of girl that should end up with a man like the one she has.

She is no longer walking the streets, but riding around with Dan Watson, her elbow resting on the truck door while they drive with the windows rolled down. The two of them at the café for lunch sometimes, the waitresses acting as if nothing could be less ordinary. The two of them stepping out of the record shop several times a week with brown-papered packages stuck under his arms. People saying, by late September, that she's picked up a second job, serving drinks to the patrons over at Las Cuatro Copas, the place where her boyfriend tends bar, and the owner of the rival place across the street is peeved because even the white crowd has trickled over there just to get a look at her.

Las Cuatro Copas isn't the best cantina in town, but if you go there, you would do well to put on your best long skirt, the wider the better because there's good music for dancing. Farther up Union Avenue is a grander space—a real nightclub—with a terrazzo dance floor so smooth you have to hang on tight to your partner to keep from slipping, and gorgeous dining rooms off to the sides with a full wait staff and a Los Angeles menu of roast beef and rib-eye steaks and Cornish hens. But Las Cuatro Copas does just fine by itself. It welcomes everyone, the little tables crowded as people sit to eat and drink until the kitchen closes at eight thirty. All the while, that girl comes around with plates of chicken legs and taquitos and bottles of beer, along with the check on a green slip of paper with her neat handwriting, and she collects the bills and brings everything over to Dan Watson, hurrying people along with their meals because the tables get put away for the dancing. Not enough space for a wide skirt to flow out full, and a wooden floor that sends up dust, but it's dancing all the same. Friday nights or Sundays or Wednesdays, she's there, handing the green slips of paper over to her boyfriend and waiting for the change, the two of them running the place smooth as smoke.

But you don't have to go to the cantina to see all of that if jealousy gets to be too much. You can avert your gaze as they exit the supermarket, where he comes out holding two paper bags stuffed full of food. Or pretend not to see them loading boxes of tequila into the truck bed over at the discount liquor store.

They show up everywhere: just a little west of Bakersfield, just far enough away from the city lights, is the local drive-in theater, a line of cars idling at the dusty entrance at sundown. A concession stand sits in the middle, and everyone goes there for big striped boxes of popcorn and hot dogs and candy, cradling everything close so only one trip is necessary. Horns beep whenever a car pulls in with its lights on, even though the sky is still lit orange with sundown and the double bill nowhere near beginning. Music comes in over the speakers, old big-band numbers that no one listens to anymore. Some couples sit out on the hoods after the engines have cooled down. The people returning from the concession stand darken to shadows as dusk finally breaks into night and the first feature starts, always something of mild interest: a monster movie with a beautiful blond raising her hands to her ears and screaming, then a pursuit with gunfire popping through the speakers all up and down the drive-in lot. Laughter carries across several cars, friends having spotted each other and walking over to say hello. Car trunks pop open quickly for six-packs to be brought out. By the end of the first film, night has settled in deep, and the drive-in lights up once more to help people make their way to the concession stand and the bathrooms, where the girls walk together in threes and edge for space at the mirrors, everyone finding out who came with whom.

She's there, that girl. You looked for her among the faces surrounding the bathroom mirrors, but she was nowhere to be found. But you know she's there—you spotted Dan Watson's beautiful form gliding across the dusty lane toward the concession stand. He returns now to his pickup, just ahead, holding a box of popcorn in his hand and sporting a cowboy hat, his jeans taut, everything lean and hard the way he glides from one end of the windshield to the other before disappearing into the cab of his truck. That girl is the other shadow. He is handing her the box. Ten minutes later, the lot darkens and the second feature begins—a detective story. You can tell by the hat the lead actor is wearing. No one wears hats like that around here, unless they're from Los Angeles. On-screen, a beautiful girl screams before a pair of anonymous hands close around her neck and she collapses as if struck by a sudden urge to sleep. She did not scream as terribly as the beautiful blond who was attacked by the monster in that other movie, but somehow it was more real, more probable, and enough to make you turn your head away and look out past the edge of the drive-in's lot, the stretch of oil fields, the ring of mountains to the south and east of Bakersfield, to Los Angeles. Is that where the movie is set, where something like this could happen?

No one seems to care about questions like that, not by how the shadows in the cars ahead begin to blend together, one by one. Some stay separate, but most don't. There's been beer and slugs of whiskey and lipstick applied in the bathroom mirror and cigarettes and sweet talk. Hands on knees and short whispers and legs shaved that evening, baby smooth. All over town, getting ready, everyone knowing—or hoping—the evening would come to this, a lot of sweet talk in a dark car and the squeak of the vinyl as your polite date slides over. The taste of the beer in his mouth, slightly bitter, but sweet, too, the surprise that men taste sweet inside. All of them. Rough but sweet. Your hand on his cheek to feel the itch of his whiskers, what you can't see but can feel. Forceful but sweet, and it's that sweetness that calms the alarm about where his hands move, sometimes above the knee or underneath the hem at the back of your blouse, just two fingertips in that hollow space at the bottom of the spine. Forceful but gentle at the same time, his mouth moving to your neck, the smell of his hair, Prell shampoo just like your own. A moan escapes from your mouth, uncontrollable, because his weight is delicious and so is the thought that he's leaving that sweet taste of his mouth on your skin. He reaches over to turn the knob down on the speaker, and the movie goes mute and you watch the screen while he's occupied, the detective at a desk saying something into a phone, how you have to guess what he's saying, the way you have to guess at everything in life—what you see and what you make of it, what you know for sure and what you have to experience, what others tell you and what gets confirmed.

You can see Dan over in his pickup truck. His shadow has merged with the other one, slipped into the same space, the passenger side of the cab. It is that girl. It must be. She knows that sweet taste, too, what that space in the hollow of his back feels like. A moan comes out of your mouth just from thinking about him, and here, in this dark car, this boy—earnest but inconsequential, strong but too sweet—hears your moan and lets his hands glide up, cautious, to the unworkable bridge of the bra hooks. There is patience and inexperience all over the drive-in, some hands retreating in defeat, and then there are others, like his, that manage and move quickly before being denied. On-screen, the detective lights a cigarette and seems to look out at all the cars. There is a woman whom the detective loves, too, but in the movie, you already know he's going to have to wait to get to her. And still, it won't be this, an earnest but inconsequential boy who is sweating at the brow from nerves and delirium, his mouth impatient at each nipple. He has never felt a pair of breasts before, not by the way his hands clamor underneath your bra. He has to learn to open the blouse completely first, how to caress buttons. He has to learn to be gentle and enjoy the feel of skin, give pleasure instead of just taking it. But right now, his eyes round out, dewy and unblinking at his first sight of rosy nipples. He is twenty-three but still a boy. He puts his mouth on each nipple and has to have his hand guided to your other breast. You reach down to feel him because this is what he wants, what he needs, and there's just the sound now of months and months of his desires finally being met. He's doing the moaning now, the teenage voice from years ago stuck in his throat as his thick cowboy belt buckle gets undone for him and the top button released. He wore brand-new underwear—the elastic is too tight—and there is his warm thickness. It's enormous and probably beautiful, but he's too young and inexperienced to know that yet. His stomach is coated with that familiar stickiness and he rests his forehead on the car door while he's fondled. Who can tell what he is thinking, a soft hand stroking him hard enough that he actually has to pull away, but keeping his forehead on the door as if he's ashamed? The detective on the screen is giving chase along the dark streets of a city, but no one cares about the pursuit. A car just ahead is bobbing ever so slightly. There is nothing wrong with wanting like this. Even better with a young man of twenty-three, still mired in shame: he won't be bragging to anyone, still thinking what he's doing is dirty, and you can go back to work at the shoe store with no one ever gossiping about you. His hands have to be brought down to the wet warmth that he's never come close to, even in his imagination, his fingers guided around and inside. He's a sweet boy, but you know, after he drops you off, that he'll be smelling those fingers all the way home.

The pickup truck is absolutely still—or is it moving? There is no telling what they are or are not doing in there. Who could push away Dan Watson? Because the speaker is off, from way over in the distance a girl's furious moans carry along the dirt lane, then some quiet laughter from people sitting on their hoods, watching the movie. Whoever heard that laughter— how people react when exposed to that kind of desire, with laughter or disgust or disapproval—might stop what they were doing. But it's happening all across the darkness, panties slipping off and resting playfully on the gearshift, on the radio knob. Yours is twenty-three and doesn't know what he's doing and he admits that he's a virgin in a terrified voice. He thrusts and it feels good only because you close your eyes and picture yourself in the pickup truck instead, the way Dan walks, the waitresses who feel dirty for thinking of him that way because they knew him when he was a little, little boy. They know his mother. You close your eyes and think of Dan but concentrate on this boy, holding him at the hips when he begins rocking too fast, getting carried away to a point when he won't be able to control himself. He's sweet in his earnestness—he truly is— and he stops when you tell him to do so, his face covered in sweat. He looks like he is about to cry.

Car engines begin to turn on even before the movie is over,

and horns blast at the disorder—some people want to know who committed the murder, who made the beautiful girl scream like that. The pickup truck stands absolutely still, the silhouettes hard to pick out now because of the shifting lights and shadows. It's time to sit back up in the seat, since people are watching now, and adjust bras, close blouses. More and more cars begin to pull out, so many there's actually a line for the exit. It is better to wait. The twenty-three-year-old boy is in love. You can tell by the way he sits there, his pants back on, but the bulge straining. He wants a kiss.

That is the difference between him and a man like Dan. This boy hasn't yet learned the power of wielding his body—giving it over—like a little boat on an ocean, the thing you cling to, getting rocked to sleep by the waves. He thinks he's in love.

And why shouldn't he, after a night like that? It's easy to think that's what love is, after being naked in front of someone for the first time, as if it truly were an act of tenderness, of sacred honor. In truth, love crumbles into something else, an answer to lying awake at two in the morning, when the body demands one thing and one thing only. The cars drive back into the sleepy streets of Bakersfield, letting off dates at the porch-lit houses, last kisses before the neighborhood dogs begin to bark at the idling engines. Soon the boy will start the hand-holding and the flowers—cheap grocery-store flowers, not Holliday's, but flowers nonetheless because that's what sweet, earnest boys do.

After October, the drive-in closes for the winter. Saturday nights become a slow circle around a little stretch of Union Avenue, the streetlights glimmering off the new wax jobs. Cars stop over at the Jolly Kone hamburger stand or at the edges of the dark city park. Winter fog keeps many people home, as if the cold were unbearable. Still, as the weeks go on, the bars begin to do substantial business, especially the ones that serve a little food early enough to draw a crowd that stays the entire evening. Traveling bands arrive in Bakersfield for special appearances, the bars competing with one another for the best of Los Angeles, sometimes even selling tickets in advance at the record shop.

In the newspaper, a little ad appears in mid-November, a curious drawing. A dark-skinned woman stands in front of a microphone. "La Reina," says the ad. "Este Domingo." And below is the address to Las Cuatro Copas. It is a drawing, not a photograph. It is that girl. Undeniably. There is something provocative about the advertisement, something deliberate about its simplicity, the fact that she is a local talent. Customers from the shoe store will surely recognize her. You leave the newspaper on the storeroom counter, conspicuous, to show her that you've seen it, but she says nothing about it. In the drawing, she stands in front of the microphone with her lips open, but who knows what might come out of her mouth. The advertisement appears again later in the week in an evening edition, same bold type, same language, same held note. At the shoe store, you swear people are peeking through the windows to get a glimpse of her. It isn't surprising when, on Sunday night, Las Cuatro Copas is packed, not one table unoccupied.

People arrive dressed as if it were a Saturday, all fine ties and shiny boots and dresses. No one licks their fingers after eating the chicken legs and taquitos, the plates carried away just as quickly as they arrived. Conversations float by in Spanish—all of them in Spanish. Some of the Mexican men have even come with blond American women, heedless of the hard glares. These couples have little to say to each other, though sometimes the women jabber on to fill the quiet space between them. Here, everyone is out in the open—it is clear who brought whom, who is being distracted, who is being worn away by jealousy, and who is going to be brokenhearted. It is not the drive-in, where the darkness lulls everyone into thinking that lust is an easy, clean jump over to the wide path of love on the other side. In the dim club, the true complications of being in love show themselves in flashes, like a wedding ring catching a burst of light. A dark-haired woman drinks too much for so early in the evening and you can tell she's trying but unable to leave the man who brought her. A very young couple sits over near the back, sitting so close together they seem almost afraid of being affected by everyone around them, and the way the young man nods at the girl when she comes around for an order—nods but doesn't say much of anything—you can tell that neither he nor his young date speak English. He is surprised that the girl takes his order in Spanish with ease. That man over there gives another woman the once-over, his hand distracted on his own date's back. Both women notice and look away in hard, granite anger.

Who knows, really, why they came tonight, if they've been paying attention to that girl and noticed her comings and goings. Who knows why they thought this evening warranted ironing a fresh shirt instead of just airing out the one from the night before, damp as it was from dancing and smoky when you put your nose to it. But here they were, their tables cleared but not stacked over in the corner as they usually were on dancing nights. Maybe later, but now just their clean tables and their chairs to sit in and a last round of drinks, the girl gone to the back of the club and the lights dimmed even further, so dark the crowd actually goes quiet and focuses on the small halo of light at the center of the cantina. So quiet you can hear the boots of the bartender boyfriend against the wood floor as he approaches the light, guitar in one hand, a microphone stand in the other, the cord snaking behind him. Someone rises from the crowd to pull over a blue velvet stool for him and Dan says thanks, tapping his fingers against the microphone. "Uno, dos, tres," he says, perfectly, which prompts an almost nervous laughter from some in the crowd. You think: He knows how to speak Spanish. He might understand what people have been saying. The microphone in working order, he waves off to the side, and out of the dark comes the waitress girl, out of her serving apron and wearing instead a beautiful cowgirl dress. Baby blue satin with white fringe. Of course, you notice that she's wearing what look like last season's brown boots, and you foolishly try to make her see that you've noticed, but your face is lost in the dark. The boots don't match the dress, but it's too dark for anyone else to really care. All eyes are on the gorgeous satin, the way it catches what little light there is, the arrow detailing beginning at her shoulder and descending, circling each breast, the silver lacing deep inside the fringe, which sparkles to attention when she adjusts the microphone.

"Ready?" she says to Dan, and that says everything to the audience: she will be singing in English, no matter what the sign said. She doesn't look anything like the picture's promise, and the Spanish nickname feels misleading. But people came because they had seen her around town with Dan Watson. Or because they knew the woman who had been her mother, or they had heard about how she'd been left to bring herself up all alone after her mother left. They came because this girl was going to sing about either love or pain, and some of them felt as if they already knew the story behind both.

People who don't know English love that Patsy Cline record from last year, all the times her song came over the radio when there was nothing else to listen to, a deep, luxurious voice for a woman, more expressive than the chirpy girl groups indistinguishable from one another. The guitar starts in and they all recognize the beginning of "Walkin' After Midnight" and the girl seems to look at the audience straight on, the first words a little quiet and her voice too high. But the couple performs the song well, the girl's hands shaking a bit before she steadies them on the microphone. She closes her eyes for a long while, as if she needs to concentrate, but then opens them again, as if she knows that she has to face everyone to feel the song. She begins to look around the room as she sings, moving her arms as if she were walking down a Bakersfield street, keeping tempo with the guitar, the song close enough to what everyone has been accustomed to on the radio. Her voice does not have the depth of Patsy Cline's, dark water swirling, but she manages to make the song tell a kind of story, as if anybody could be walking down the late-night streets of Bakersfield, haunted by that searching, but hopeful about it, no danger whatsoever. People nod their heads along to the guitar's polite strum, the English words familiar, the way English becomes familiar enough with repetition, her fringe dancing, glittering along.

For the second number, after small but prolonged applause, the girl almost turns her back to them to look at her boyfriend as he begins the first notes. Everyone sees him motion her to turn around, reminding her that she has an audience, and so she positions herself in a sideways posture, a little awkward, but it is clear what is going to happen. She needs to face him, and the notes off the guitar sing to the audience in a prolonged introduction, the melody immediately familiar to some, others needing to wait for the words. It is clear what is going to happen: they are going to sing to each other, her boyfriend a little hidden in the dark, away from the half-moon of the spotlight. And now everyone has something to privately admire: the shape of Dan's muscular thigh perched off the stool, tapping in tune; the girl's still-trembling hand on the microphone; Dan's superb coordination over the guitar strings; the girl's narrow, beautiful waist. They begin singing the song and right away the people who need the words remember the Everly Brothers and their shiny innocence, their politely combed hair. But tonight, "All I Have to Do Is Dream" comes over as a different song altogether—not two brothers and teenage heartbreak, but a more adult, public affirmation. The girl wavers but stays on the slow, hopeful tempo, watching her boyfriend, who sings back to her in a surprising tenor. This is love. This is what it is supposed to be like—a handsome man and a girl who comes from nothing, and now everything changes because he has arrived. A girl becomes a woman, devoted at last because her man has exhibited the courage to be tender. That's the way you hear the song, as a shopgirl in a small city, and you see that it all depends on who is listening and why, who grasps a date's hand in the dark as the song goes on, who knows what the words were actually saying.

Just two songs. Nothing worth the grand pronouncement of an advertisement in the paper. He was a better singer than she was and even played the guitar, but he stands away from the circle of spotlight and allows her to take her bows. "¡Bravo!" call out some of the Spanish-speaking men. "¡Bravo!" As if they understood every word, as if they didn't notice Dan Watson making a proprietary motion around her delicate waist when she moves toward the back of the cantina. They cheer her all the way out, for just two songs, as if she has fulfilled whatever promise the advertisement in the newspaper suggested, her embrace of the microphone, of them, the dark beauty of her skin, her face, her voice.

After the tables are stacked, the dancing begins, a lot of ballads in both English and Spanish to keep the mood going, the women falling into their men's arms, heads on shoulders and eyes closed. You do the same to your date, his shoulder too thin to carry your defeat. People could think you were in love with this boy, maybe imagine it was something close to that girl and the bartender, resonant and tremulous. But you can only close your eyes in disappointment that the smell of the neck you've nestled into is of Ivory soap, of Prell shampoo and no cologne, one of the Everly Brothers and not that man. Sweet pronouncements have their place, but no man should be singing about a broken heart, about longing. He should be there to fix it, the way Dan sang tonight, the words saying one thing but his thigh on the stool saying another, his longing a stage act because he already has what he desired.

With your eyes closed, you think of what it will be like to go back to work at the shoe store, working alongside that girl, how hard it will be not to seem jealous about every good thing that has come her way. It won't be long before she quits the job altogether, stepping through the doorway never to return, leaving you to go through the days without any exit of your own.

Your head is heavy on your date's shoulder. People dance for a short while, but the cantina begins to empty by eleven o'clock. It is a Sunday night after all and tomorrow morning is work. But the routine for the night seems to have been set, more or less. November rolls on and again the same advertisement appears in the paper and the picture begins to make sense to people: La Reina has a story to tell, but you have to listen to the songs she chooses in order to understand it. You have to put a story together against what you might already have heard on the street about her. The songs will tell you how she's become a queen, has become fit to be treated like one. You have to watch her sing to Dan, and know that he doesn't care where she comes from or who her family is. People begin to come in more and more, deep into November, on into December, convinced that she'll sing a song that explains her stage name or even something in Spanish to prove she knows it, the way her boyfriend taps the microphone at the beginning of their two-song sets, "Uno, dos, tres."

The cold fog settles into Bakersfield, and even in the worst of its thickness, the cars prowl out along Union Avenue and maneuver into the gravel parking lot, ladies shivering in their dresses and short jackets. Maybe tonight she will sing "I Only Have Eyes for You." Their love is bigger than yours, truer, headed for a certain destination. It is wiping away jealousy and loneliness with nothing but song and sincerity, the simplicity of it almost unfair. You can listen as she sings "Tears on My Pillow," but the truth of her world makes the song cruel to hear, the will to sacrifice the heart all over again with possibly nothing in return, the heart never forgetting. How could this be true for her? Her boyfriend is right there, even if he is in the dark, and never leaving, so she can sing all the loneliness she wants. It will never touch her.

In December, the ads keep appearing, but with Christmas coming and New Year's Eve and the general lack of work out in the fields, the cantina begins to slow down a bit. Still, there is the ad, something to look at on a Sunday night when there will be no going out, when the sweet but earnest twenty-three-year-old is left breathless on the phone when he is told no. La Reina opens her soul out on the page, familiar to many now. A hard rain begins that night and lasts all through the morning, steady, the clouds lingering over the Pacific Ocean for days before swirling in. When next week's edition of the paper is thrown on the doorstep, the paperboy misses his target and it lands in a bush. The paper soaks through. Because there is nothing else to do, the rain keeping everyone indoors, you lay the paper out on the kitchen table to dry in the steamed-up warmth of the house. The ink has run, but parts are salvage-able, the news of the entire city spread out for inspection.

There, on page 3, is a picture of the bowling alley over near Chester Avenue, a police officer standing in front. There is the girl's name in the text. There is Dan Watson's. Page 1 is ink-smeared from the rain and nearly impossible to read, but it is clear something terrible has happened. She was twenty-three.

There is what you see and what you make of it, what you know for sure and what you have to experience, what others tell you and what gets confirmed.

Phone calls ricochet all around town. The rain keeps most people from venturing out, or else speculation would be the subject at every bar, every coffee shop, every diner and café. She lived in the apartment above the bowling alley and was a quiet girl, according to the landlord's account in the newspaper. On the night the rainstorm began, said some who claimed to have been in the cantina the very night she was killed, the two of them had a terrible fight. Others said that never happened, that the couple had been seen at the movies. The stairwell up to her apartment had a side wall smeared in blood, someone said. The newspaper reported she had been beaten to death. You can kill someone with your bare hands. A man can kill a woman that way. Even a sweet, earnest boy is capable of that, if he thinks about it, if he recognizes his power, his weight, his thrust, his fists coming down. On page 8 of the paper, the ad-vertisement for Las Cuatro Copas still runs, La Reina with her mouth open.

She had been stealing money. She had been pregnant with

his child. She had been caught with another man. The landlord refuses to rent the apartment. He cannot get the blood off
the wall.

There is what you see and what you make of it: You know
she stole those boots from the store's inventory. You know for
sure. You can confirm it by the totals coming up short in the
ledger. But you keep that to yourself.

Dan Watson disappears, and by the time the newspaper re-
ports this, it is old news, if news at all. The newspaper cannot
say anything except that the situation is under investigation.
The rain clears up and patrons in the café discuss it with the
waitresses when Dan's mother is not on shift. They scoff at
the paper, calling it a situation and not a murder. Someone calls
the paper and admonishes them for having run the cantina's
advertisement. But there are still some who don't know that the
girl and La Reina are one and the same.

You can hear people discuss it as December goes on, but no
one goes into the uglier details. Was there really blood on the
wall? At the drive-in movie, the beautiful woman was strangled
to death, but she slumped over as if in a sudden sleep. Music
thrummed ominously. At the drive-in movie, boys and men
undid bras and pulled off panties, eager to get to the wet warmth
underneath the skirts. Maybe not every girl let them. There
was that one who moaned hard, enjoying it, and the laughter
from people sitting on the hoods of their cars. But not every girl
was like that. Not every girl allowed that. Maybe Dan never did
that with her at the drive-in. The landlord said she was a nice
girl. You could see how she sang, how she chose songs that were
always about love, Dan stepping out of the record shop with

brown-papered packages. But then again, all the songs nowadays were about love, whether you lost it or found it or gave it away.

At the café, no one talks about it when Dan's mother is on shift. No one can imagine what it is like to be the mother of a man like that. All the waitresses who flirted with him can only talk about remembering him when he was a little, little boy.

The rain lets up and is promptly replaced by the fog. There are Mexican men at the corner grocery store near the girl's apartment, waiting every morning for fieldwork. They sit watching people driving by slowly to get a look at the splintered green door that opens to that stairwell, or at the dark window of the girl's apartment. They watch people actually go up to the door and try the knob. Her face was beaten so badly, goes the story around town, that there was a closed casket. Others say she had no funeral at all, that she was just buried in what they call the public side of the city cemetery because she didn't have any people in Bakersfield.

She was twenty-three. The cemetery put a little marker about the size of a fist over in a corner lot—TERESA GARZA—because city regulations mandate that no graves go unmarked.

In late December, Dan Watson is nowhere to be found. Later, the police detain one of the Mexican men from across the street, that bunch of men who sit around the corner grocery waiting for work. That man, people say, was another boyfriend, but by this point, no one really knows the story anymore. The rest of the Mexican workers scatter for days, not returning, but it doesn't matter. By January, work is scarce. All of Bakersfield has to tighten its wallet as the thick of winter settles in.

Hardly anyone comes to the shoe store, even out of curiosity, and you rest your elbows on the counter and count the days until spring. The Mexican man is deported, but the newspaper never says why—that's something you hear only on the street. All winter long, the splintered green door remains locked, a strange brightness in the dull of the January fog.

Two

The Actress was set to arrive in Bakersfield in the morning. She would be driven from Los Angeles, picked up from the studio at 6 a.m. sharp in a black sedan, and carried over the mountains into the city of Bakersfield to meet with the Director. She was a dedicated actress, script in hand as the sedan wound its way out of the quiet Los Angeles morning, a croissant and a carton of juice to sate her appetite. The driver respected her need for silence, her head bent over the script. She fought the nausea of reading against the car's steady thrum.

The Director had told her explicitly not to worry much about the entire script: they were shooting only two exterior shots, coming quietly into Bakersfield without a lot of fanfare, and the rest would be filmed at a Los Angeles studio. The Actress already knew her lines, but it never hurt to read again or to review scenes that had nothing to do with her. The exteriors were to be shot on the outskirts of the city, somewhere along Highway 99: A woman is driving a car on a road, all alone. The woman has no one to talk to, hence the Actress had no real lines to rehearse. But the Actress knew, at the very least, that her facial expressions would have to match the mood of the final edit, would have to match what she saw in the parentheticals scattered all over the script: there would be voice-overs, something else telling the story besides her own face.

She put down the script and watched the slope of the hills roll by in the October morning light. Excursions like these—trips to actual locations, away from the studio lot, all in the name of authenticity—made her wonder about the fuss, whether it was much of a role at all. The Actress had two children and a husband at home. Luckily, most of this film was scheduled to shoot in Los Angeles; it was becoming too difficult to get away from the city for work. The roles had to be studio-shot for her to be able to accept them, but these days that meant only the smaller pictures or television. Color was splashing across enormous screens and that meant directors wanted to go out to the Painted Desert, to the skyscrapers of New York City, even Japan—the real thing, not a backdrop, had to appear on the screen. At first, she believed it to be nothing more than the directors and the studios wanting to show off their enormous budgets, but the films coming over from Europe flashed with a bold realism that signaled a readiness to deepen the craft. Even the actresses appeared as if they were hauled in from the street, frighteningly believable and fully invested in their roles, not a hint of studio training in their performances. Maybe they were not even actresses at all, but authentics: a housewife, a drunk, a gold digger, a prostitute.

She had her own doubts about her ability. Sometimes she wondered if she hadn't been born twenty years too late, the way she'd been ushered in, discovered when she was up north in the Valley, way past Bakersfield, at the little college where she had modeled. Ushered in: a little star on a string, handshakes with the right people, a contract to sign, scripts to read, and her cooperation at every turn. In exchange, a whole bevy of people hovered around her: hair stylists and publicists, women who led her to Los Angeles department stores for personal fittings, awards ceremony appearances. A whole other life that had nothing to do with acting, nothing to do with any realism, nothing on the level of those European actresses, who came from places rising up out of the rubble of the war and knew a thing or two about stories.

Her scene today would be a woman driving a car, not a word said to anyone. Tomorrow, a character actor would arrive for a scene to be shot somewhere to the east of this very road she was traveling, maybe out by Lancaster. In the scene, the woman has pulled over to the side of the road to sleep for the night, only to be awakened in the morning by a policeman, who knocks on her window and questions her. At most, a three-minute scene, but there was a crucial signpost for Gorman, California, the Director had told them, some signal to the audience that this woman was headed north. Did it matter that no one knew Gorman? She knew it, the little stop-off point for the traffic snaking through the Grapevine from the Valley on through to the Los Angeles area. Almost anyone in Los Angeles would probably know that. But would an audience member in New York City know, or even care?

The Actress wasn't supposed to ask those questions, and she smirked at herself dismissively, looking out the window. It wasn't her place to ask. She had a task at hand and nothing more. A silent scene of nervousness just this side of panic. Yes, she thought. That was exactly how she would play it.

It was easy, she knew, and maybe even halfway logical, for an audience to think a film was shot scene by ordered scene. That's how life worked, after all, one thing happening after another. But this picture was being done piecemeal, a haphazard schedule. She had to think hard about the story. She found it difficult to follow the script sometimes, forgetting where the scene was placed in the story's arc, what her character did or did not know. But she held her tongue and chided herself: she knew exactly what the Director would tell her. *You hold in your hands a script. It tells you everything you need to know. If it's not there, you don't need to know it.*

She looked up at the October sky over the hills, completely and unsurprisingly blue. Would the weather hold? No rain was expected, not even cloud cover, no worries for tomorrow. Just the technicalities of a short location shoot, away from the city itself and no onlookers: the equipment, the crew, the two actors. All for a scene that wouldn't take place until well into the movie's first act. But that was the beauty of editing, the layered splices after so many takes, a story without a seam. Such was her responsibility, to suggest continuity without effort, every scene making its crucial contribution, even though she had little to say. She looked at the script again and pictured how the shooting would go. First, the scene shot with a camera near the driver's side window. Then the scene shot again with the camera crowding into her by the passenger seat. Then the shots again for line delivery, for lighting, for the position of the actor playing the policeman, for the microphones, for the position of her hands on the steering wheel, for the lighting director to adjust his reflective screens as the sun slowly made its way through morning. Again and again and again.

For such a small role. She wasn't going to be in the picture after the first third. When the Actress had first read the script, she stopped on the character's fate, then flipped back to the first page and the cast of characters. She was going to disappear. Violently. She tried to pay no mind to how the Director might have to stage this particular scene, focused only on the end of her character, the bulk of the script's pages still gripped in the fingers of her right hand.

A supporting role. Nothing more. In the Director's previous picture, that one actress had appeared playing two roles. She hadn't done a particularly stellar job, some in the industry had said, but the Actress thought the performance more than adequate. She had sat in the theater with mild envy, the role too rich for words: A distraught wife is trailed silently throughout San Francisco by a police detective, from flower shop to museum to the foot of the glorious Golden Gate Bridge, where she finally tries to hurl herself into the bay. The detective rescues her and later falls in love, only to lose her again to a successful suicide attempt. It played, the Actress thought, like an odd type of silent movie, and she felt maybe she had fooled herself into believing she could have fit perfectly into the part. Was it really requiring much beyond posing, or was there something about silent-movie acting that she didn't know? She wondered what the script must have looked like, that other actress—who couldn't have been professionally trained—skimming the pages until she found her first line.

No matter how small the role was going to be, it would have been foolish to say no to the Director. He was in the midst of doing something extraordinary and uncanny with some actresses, finessing their star wattage and burnishing it into a singular, almost iconic image. That was the way the Actress saw it anyway, mesmerized by how he was stripping out all the trappings of the industry and pushing these women toward something beyond even acting, something nakedly cinematic—postures, poses, gestures, as if the women were in magazine ads come to life for just split seconds at a time, just enough motion for the public to remember them as images and not characters. It was like opening up a jewelry box she had had many years ago as a young girl, fascinated by the tiny plastic ballerina in the center and its brief circle of motion. She had closed and opened that box endlessly, even though the ballerina did nothing differently. But even now, in a black sedan carrying her over the Grapevine back toward the Valley, where she had grown up, the Actress could close her eyes and remember the golden lace of the ballerina's costume, the full circle of her deliciously patient twirl, her perfect timing with the delicate chime of the music box's single tune. And that was the way the screen worked, too, she had discovered. Every actress's trajectory carried a moment like that, and the Director was staging them effortlessly.

She could feel the car's engine release a little—the upward climb was ending, and the road was leveling out briefly before the inevitable decline. She peered over the bench seat to get a look out the front window, but so far they hadn't reached a place where she could see the horizon of the Valley stretching out before them.

"We're almost there, ma'am," the driver said. "Probably another hour or so."

"Oh, I hope I didn't look impatient," she said. "There's a point in the road where you can see for miles across. I thought I had missed it."

"You've been on this road before, ma'am?"

"Absolutely. Does that surprise you?"

"Well, mostly it's people going the other way," the driver said. "Getting away from Bakersfield, Fresno, all those little towns in between. Everyone wants to go to Los Angeles. I don't see any reason why anybody would be going into the Valley."

"Fruit buyers. Cotton. Oilmen, too. There's money to be made down there."

"You're a smart lady. I'm from the Valley, you know, and most people don't think of this place that way."

She said nothing in response for a moment, not wanting to reveal much about herself. She had learned to be careful over the years. She studied the back of the driver's head, his careful concentration on the road. "I was born here," she finally offered, "over past Fresno."

"Is that right?" he said, meeting her eyes in the rearview mirror. "I'm from Stockton myself, born and raised."

"Do you still have family there?"

"Yes, ma'am. My parents are still there, but they're getting on in years."

She smiled at him when he glanced at her in the mirror, but

did not respond. But the silence wasn't awkward. He went back to the task at hand; she knew how the studios laid down the law on drivers, on crew, even on extras. She studied the back of his head, a handsome square with a clean line from a fresh haircut. Ever so slightly now, the sedan was beginning to pick up speed, the road taking a gradual slope downward, but she resisted leaning forward again to catch a view.

"I hope you won't think I'm being nosy," said the driver, "but I hardly think you're on your way to do a musical."

She laughed a little and shook her head. "No, nothing like that. Not in Bakersfield."

"Well, it is a big music city, you know. Lots of country. I'm sure there's a good story in there somehow. With a country music star and all."

"Maybe," she replied. "But you couldn't see me as a cowgirl, could you?"

"I sure could!" He was beginning to take his eyes off the road just a bit much for her comfort, but there wasn't going to be a way to return to the silence of before without seeming rude. She could feel the pull of the road downward. "I tell you what—you'd make a prettier cowgirl than that Elizabeth Taylor."

"That's very kind of you to say," she said, then leaned up to look at the road. They were most definitely on the way down the slope of the Grapevine, but the road curved here and there and the full, unobstructed view of the Valley had yet to come. They went silent again, and she looked once more at the driver's clean hairline, the square rigidity, and then let her eyes travel briefly down the slope of his shoulder.

This girl is in love with a divorced man and will do anything for him, she'd been told, but the direction had ended right there during the read-through. *This girl.* A read-through, not a rehearsal. Silently, she had sat at the table with the Director and the other actors and asked herself if she knew what it would be like to love another woman's ex-husband, but the script said nothing about shame, about moral obligations, nothing about right or wrong. And the Director had long ago put his foot down on any shenanigans about character, about Method, about needing quiet spaces before a scene started: this was a job, not a psychiatric couch.

She pictured running her finger along the edge of the driver's shoulder and wondered if his eyes would register complicity when they looked up to meet hers in the rearview mirror.

Is that how the European actresses did it, how they lost themselves in their scripted terrors?

You have beautiful eyes, said the woman who had discovered her years ago, a silent-film star. *It's all in the eyes.*

"I'm not exaggerating, ma'am. My wife and I both admire you very much, especially in the movies where you sing and dance. You're an absolutely talented lady. First class! We think you're just wonderful!"

"Thank you," the Actress replied, and the moment she said it, she wished she could have given the words more than the note of resignation underneath. She wondered if she had betrayed what she had been thinking just by speaking aloud, and this worried and thrilled her at the same time: it was a private knowledge she wanted to hone, to use during the filming, in order to practice at being a real actress, to use every available tool. Her voice, her eyes, her fluttering tone. That would be all she could control. Everything else, she was beginning to suspect, would be modeled for her.

The driver went quiet again, his eyes back on the road, and she felt sorry for not taking in his pleasure, his willingness to give her praise, even though she had long ago discarded the need for adulation, that small bird singing inside. It was one thing to enter this business for that very reason—she could be honest with herself about that—but it was quite another to let that feeling guide her well-being. She had come from this very Valley to Hollywood as a starlet—a dancer and singer with enough talent not to embarrass anyone—but that was over ten years ago now, and somewhere along the line, she had realized the adoration would not last very long. She should drink it in, every chance she had.

You have beautiful eyes, the silent-film star had told her, as if there were an urgency in using them, as if the silent-film star herself had never noticed anyone taking an indiscreet glance at her lazy eye, drooping a little when she had too much champagne.

"Look," said the driver. "There's your view."

The Actress leaned forward and there it was: the long green Valley flanked on the west by the low coastal hills, over on the east by the towering Sierra, the place she had been born in, had come from, maybe was destined to return to. "Majestic, isn't it?" she said. "Gorgeous, really."

"Yes, ma'am. From the Lord's point of view, everything looks beautiful."

The road was level, but she could feel the sedan picking up

speed. The descent would start soon, and with it the curving roads. She felt her stomach drop heavy for a moment even before they began going down, the Valley beckoning below.

Are you willing to wear only a brassiere for the opening scene? The Director had asked her. *It's important for the atmosphere.*

Fruit. Cotton. Oil. The land spread out as far as she could see. The story of the woman would take place in the Valley, but there was no landmark to let the audience know. No leaning tower, no red bridge, no streets of stark white monuments. It was a terrible story to tell.

Ma'am, I know where I can have you fitted for some black brassieres, a wardrobe mistress assured her. *Very elegant, very discreet.*

The script made no claim on morals, on shame, on right or wrong. But there were white brassieres and black ones, a black purse matched by a white one. What for, if only to signal the audience? Were things ever so clear in real life?

In the story, there was a sister. She kept her clothes on. The Actress wondered about that role, if maybe it wasn't the one she should be playing.

The road started down, and just as she suspected, her stomach sank. She wanted to lean back into her seat and not look ahead, where the view of the majestic Valley dipped away from their sight, obscured by the hills as the road dove down their descent. The curves began making her feel nauseated and regretful of the orange juice and croissant she'd had for breakfast, but the Actress remained leaning forward, one hand on the bench seat, feeling a little proud of her bravery as the driver negotiated the turns.

The girl will do anything. She steals the money and runs.

She could not ask the Director. She only asked herself, silently. What is it like to love a man who left his wife, who is still angry at her? What is it like to steal money? What is it like to run? What is it like to know you've made an error, to know you've acted in complete haste? What is it like to have a police officer arrest you? What is it like to know there might not be a turning back?

Would she do anything?

In my opinion, the girl should bare her breasts in the opening scene. It would tell the audience everything about how tawdry and put-upon this girl is. But we're behind the times. Oh, now, I can see by that look on your face that you wouldn't have done a nude scene. Rest assured that I would never have asked you to do so. But in ten years' time, I do believe it will be fairly common practice, don't you agree? Don't you think the European girls will show us their bare breasts before the Americans?

The feeling in her stomach lightened. The road had only a few curves left, but already she could see that the hills were giving way, as if they were gates of some kind, and the Valley opened up before them, Bakersfield now a straight shot along the flat, dry road.

"Thank you," the Actress said, and she put her hand on the driver's shoulder. She could feel his strength through her fingertips. "I appreciate getting here safely."

Three

Around town, she was known as Mrs. Watson, even though the badge on her pink waitress uniform told everyone at the café that her name was Arlene. She was the woman with the brown hair in a tight bun and a mouth set in a hard straight line. "Mrs. Watson" had always sounded old to her, a schoolmarm name, even if people used it with respect. A schoolmarm, though not as old as one. But she had worked there so long that people assumed she was older than she was. She had first started back in 1946—thirteen years ago now—but even then, when she was only thirty-four years old, people called her Mrs. Watson.

They called her that because they knew her husband, Frederick, one of the first proprietors of a business out by Highway 99, a motel built with his own hands, one wing at a time. He had been young when he put up the motel—only in his thirties—and yet people called him Mr. Watson out of respect. They admired his prescience when the roads toward Los Angeles were later improved by the state. More trucks, more produce, more barrels of oil, more chickens, more hogs. All of those drivers needed a place to sleep and they stopped at Watson's Inn.

What a sharp business mind—and for someone so young. All around town he was greeted as Mr. Watson, as sir. Only his close friends called him Frederick.

It was as if he'd been two people, one before and one after, but she knew he was the same person all along, the same Frederick. She, too, was the same Arlene. Her maiden name had been Watson, so when she stood, all those years ago, in Bakersfield's city hall with a rough bouquet of home-garden zinnias, hardly anything changed. She married Frederick Watson, no relation, his side of the family from Wisconsin and hers from Oklahoma, with no stray cousins in between. She had stood in front of the municipal judge for hardly ten minutes and then stepped away with the same name. Arlene Watson. Except now, as Frederick's wife, she had no first name.

That morning at the café had been like most, busy very early past dawn, then a second wave around eight thirty, then a short lull before lunch. Because it was October, the high school students who helped on occasion weren't around to fill out shifts; Arlene and the rest of the waitresses had to hustle to turn over tables. By now, though, they'd all grown used to it, the students having settled back into school around Labor Day. Six weeks of this schedule, or maybe a little more, but things were changing. The light, for one. The harshness of the summer was over and the full plate-glass windows let in the softer hue of the Valley's autumn sunlight, nothing to squint against, and no more need to draw down the shades. The farmers were relaxing a bit more, the last of the summer harvesting being shipped away, and they lingered around for extra cups of coffee.

"Mrs. Watson . . ." One of her regulars, a young farmer's son named Cal, spread the newspaper on the counter and pointed at an article. "Talk's been going on for a while about this new highway to replace the old Ninety-nine. You worried about that?"

She put down her pot of coffee and leaned her head over, as if to read the article for the very first time, as if she hadn't scanned it at the crack of dawn in the office of Watson's Inn, biting her lip.

"Now why would I worry?" Arlene asked.

"That highway goes up, you'd have to rebuild, won't you? Who would stop at your motel?"

"Those things take years," she answered, wiping down the counter, busying herself as she had all morning with nervous tidying. Sometimes Cal forgot his manners and wore his hat indoors, as he was doing today. He was young. She reached up and removed the hat for him, as she had been wanting to do all morning long.

He put his hand sheepishly on the hat but made no apology, keeping his finger on the newspaper. She had wanted the gesture to be playful, a suggestion that she was approachable and not just the one among the older waitresses with a hard line for a mouth, but Cal had offered no real reaction, as if she'd never done anything at all. He focused his attention back on the paper. "They say right here, though—"

Vernon, one of the older farmers, hushed him. "Cal, just because she's pouring coffee doesn't mean she's not a smart lady."

"I don't mean it like that . . ."

"All that highway talk is mixed up in a whole mess in federal funding and state regulations up in Sacramento that will take years to sort," said Vernon. "She's got time to figure something out."

"I'm not worried about it right now, Cal," she said. She poured him some more coffee, though truth was, she wouldn't mind if he picked up and went off to work for what remained of the morning. She certainly had seen the article; it hadn't been the first time that mention of the highway had come across the pages.

"Time moves fast," said Cal, grabbing sugar.

"What do you know about time moving fast?" Vernon said. "What are you, twenty years old or thereabouts?"

"I'm twenty-three."

When Vernon laughed, he looked over at Arlene as if for approval, and she smiled broadly at him, chagrined a little for Cal despite his meaning well. This is what she liked about Vernon. He was one of the few who seemed to understand that she was someone beyond her last name, someone beyond Frederick's former wife. She knew how, behind her back, people talked about how Frederick had left her. She knew that. It was that kind of town.

"You need anything else?" she asked Vernon.

"Some pie," he said. "Slow morning, so I may as well linger. Make it cherry."

"Cal?"

"No, ma'am," he answered, not raising his head.

Back in the kitchen, some of the younger waitresses passed the morning lull leaning up against the counters and flipping through copies of *Modern Screen*, cigarettes held over the sink.

Had it been summer, Arlene would've clapped her hands to rush them back to work: she wasn't the manager, but she was the oldest on shift, and they treated her as such, hushing their back-and-forth chitchat whenever she entered the kitchen, blushing if she shook her head disapprovingly at someone's pleasure in getting playfully grabbed by one of the farmers. When the summer crew was around, she felt a keen sense of their being only girls. She was forty-seven years old and their chatter made her feel every bit of it. She watched them gather around the magazine when one sighed approvingly at a photo-graph, but paid them no mind as she prepared Vernon's cherry pie. Vernon might tease Cal for his naïveté, but he wasn't lim-ited like these girls. He wasn't like them, incapable of pushing past lazy daydreaming. He was absolutely right about things changing. How someone so young could know such a thing. She wanted to show them how things change before you real-ize they have. The café's plate-glass windows, which reached from ceiling to sidewalk, had survived the '52 earthquake, and over the years even the view from them had changed. Across the street, a beautiful flower shop called Holliday's had opened one spring, complete with an arbor over the front door. Shady, so the flowers and the potted plants could benefit from the open air even as the Valley's wilting summer heat arrived. The TG&Y expanded, taking over a local five-and-dime, the walls between the stores torn down and the buildings merged, so now you could pull drawers of Simplicity dress patterns and pick your own fabric from a rainbow of bolts lined all in a row. Things change. A wave of tract houses went up over on the east side, every one with a wide lawn. An RCA color TV sat in the window of Stewart's Appliances for only three weeks, gleaming and expensive, and someone actually had the money to buy it. The farmhouse where she had grown up blew down in a bad storm years and years ago.

"That's a big hunk of pie," said one of the girls. She puffed on her cigarette. "Is Farmer Jones staying through lunch?"

"If it's for Cal, I'll serve it to him," said another.

"You girls hush before your voices carry," Arlene admonished them. She walked out with the cherry pie and set it before Vernon Jones, who nodded his thanks. Cal remained concentrated on his newspaper, unaware of both Arlene and the sneaking glances of the younger waitresses peering through the round window of the swinging kitchen door. He wasn't an unattractive young man—studious and hardworking, as most of the farmers' sons tended to be—but it would take a few more years until he grew into the rugged assurance of someone like Vernon Jones. Cal was the same age as her own Dan, but her son's demeanor and confidence were years past Cal's—qualities she had seen her son grasp from a very young age, when as a little boy he had received the cooing attention from the other waitresses whenever she brought him along to pick up a paycheck. He'd been lanky as a teenager, but that hadn't stopped the attention from becoming downright embarrassing, to the point that she'd asked Dan not to bring his dates to the café.

These days, he'd been seen around town with the Mexican girl who worked over the shoe store. Some of the dimmer young waitresses made mention of Dan's lunch with his young date, not noting the displeasure on Arlene's face, but she made herself look busy and ignored the comments. She knew any of the waitresses would scramble to get to his table, even with her on watch, but Dan had been sensible enough to understand that he wasn't to bring that girl around while she was working.

Vernon ate his cherry pie with contentment, taking a side glance out to the sidewalk. He appeared in no hurry, but he also kept his head bent, and Arlene engaged him no further in conversation. Cal kept reading every last line of the local news and even flipped back to the front page to start the task all over again. Lunch was approaching, but for the time being, Arlene let the girls in the back hover around their *Modern Screen* while she prepped some of the tables for the lunch rush.

When the man and the woman walked in, Arlene noticed first the woman's brilliant yellow blouse. It was difficult not to think of the deep yellow tucked in the corner of a children's drawing, an extraordinary sun, and she knew instantly that this woman was not from town. Even at a distance, she could tell the blouse was expensive.

"A table?" the man said when Arlene stood looking at them, a cleaning rag in hand.

"Yes," she answered. "This way, please." She pointed them to a booth she had just cleaned, holding the cleaning rag behind her back as she reached to the counter for two menus.

"Is it too late for breakfast?" the man asked.

"Not at all," Arlene said. "I'll get you both some coffee."

"Tea for me," said the woman.

"Yes, ma'am."

When Arlene walked away, the woman's voice lingered with her, its lilt and melody. The woman had looked up, just briefly, but it was only now, back in the kitchen, that Arlene set down two cups and realized the woman was not from the town at all. She looked over at the other waitresses, still not bored with their *Modern Screen,* and it was when she saw the magazine cover that she thought of that other world over the mountains, over in Los Angeles, and knew that the woman had come from there. She wondered if the girls would've recognized the woman the minute she opened the door.

Her realization unspooled an unease. She had a habit of watching cups and glasses when they were filled to their tops, trying to walk as smoothly as possible so none of the liquid would spill over and make a mess. But this time, heading back to the table, the brightness of the woman's yellow blouse brought Arlene to near distraction, and she had to set the cups down on the counter before the couple could see, and swipe the edges clean where some of the tea had spilled. The couple didn't notice her and neither did Vernon or Cal, whose backs were turned to the booths. Vernon, in fact, was rising and reaching for his wallet to pay his familiar tab.

"Bye, now," Vernon said, and stepped out the door, just as Arlene was setting the cups down. She was too focused on setting them down and not spilling again that by the time she could raise her head to return his good-bye, the door had already closed.

"What can I get you?" she asked. Without hesitation, the man ordered a full breakfast, but the woman took her time, her eyes down on the menu, and while she did so, Arlene looked closer at her yellow blouse. It was made of silk, right down to the round crafted buttons.

"Just toast and tea," the woman said.

Arlene didn't bother to write it down and took their menus. "Pardon me," she said, "but does anyone ever tell you that you look like—"

The woman interrupted her with a wave of her hand and a shy, almost nervous smile. "Oh, no! Not in the least."

"You mean no one tells you?"

"No, I mean I don't think I look like her at all."

Cal turned around in the commotion, and the woman gave him a glance but brought her eyes right back to Arlene. She held them there, smiling politely, but offered no response. She wouldn't take her eyes off Arlene. Finally, she asked, "Is there something wrong?"

"No, ma'am," said Arlene. But as she walked away, she muttered, "The spitting image," regretting it instantly. The words came out low, almost under her breath, maybe even with a note of unintended hostility—here was the perception about her all over again, the way she carried herself, but now with people who didn't even live in the city. She wasn't a mean, cheerless person at all, just exhausted, unable to summon the spirited smiles of the young waitresses, the way they pitched their voices high and loud and sunny, always enough to turn a whole table of men deep in conversation to answer back. It was difficult to balance her tone or the need to smile, like trying to remember to correct her posture, trying to stand straight as a dancer.

She could hear Cal swivel the stool, back to his paper, as she made her way back to the kitchen to hand in their order. The girls had finished both the magazine and the cigarettes and had been busy standing around. When one of them saw Arlene, the girl pulled her hip away from the counter and slung her apron off

her shoulder to get back to work. Arlene wished she wouldn't—
she'd see the couple out at the table—but in pretending to look
rushed, she prompted the girl to hustle even more.

"Hey," the girl said, looking through the door's round window, "that's my station."

"I don't mind, Priscilla," said Arlene.

"I didn't go over my break or anything," said Priscilla. "It's
not like I was late."

"I'll throw you the tip," said Arlene.

"He's handsome," said Priscilla. "How come the men in
town don't dress like him?"

The cook rang the bell and pushed over the man's breakfast
plate.

"He's a big eater," said Priscilla, and before Arlene could stop
her, she grabbed his plate and scurried toward the door, gig-
gling at Arlene as she passed through.

The woman's toast came next, and Arlene cut two small
squares of butter as quickly as she could, rushing out to the
table. As she'd guessed, Priscilla must have recognized the
woman's face right away: she stood with her hand on her hip,
her mouth open in a wide, disbelieving smile as the woman
shook her head.

"Your toast, miss," said Arlene. "Thanks, Priscilla. Is there
anything else we can get you?"

"No, ma'am, we're fine," said the man, raising his utensils
and holding them over the plate.

Arlene put her hand on Priscilla's arm. Priscilla looked as
if she was about to ignore the man's signal. "Let's let them eat
now."

It took no time at all for Priscilla to report back to the rest, and Arlene shushed them when they all gathered at the kitchen door to have a look for themselves. "It may or it may not be her," she said to them in a harsh whisper. "But behave yourselves. It's all about grace."

"That's not her," someone said. "That's not her husband."

"She's too busty."

"There's no such thing as too busty."

"Grab the magazine," someone else said. "I think there was a picture of her in there, no?"

"That's not her husband," someone said again.

"You big dummy, if she's having an affair, that's exactly why she's here and not in Hollywood."

"Girls," Arlene said firmly. "Enough. Get away from that door."

"We have to get back to work anyway," someone said. "The lunch rush is coming."

"Fine," said Arlene, but she moved in front of them to block the door. "But no gawking. Whether it's her or not, it's embarrassing to act like a bunch of teenagers when you're supposed to be working."

None of the girls answered back, but she could tell by their folded arms and pursed lips that they resented her tone. Still, each of them gathered an apron or a tray of condiments or a dishrag or a handful of clean silverware and fanned out among the tables and booths. She could see some of them trying to take a good look at the couple, but none of the girls did so obtrusively, the couple involved as they were in their conversation. They were left alone, and as the lunch crowd began to filter in, the girls took to their tables and Arlene positioned herself behind the counter. Cal paid his bill silently and tipped his hat at her pointedly, and after he exited, she had a clear view of the couple as they chatted, the gorgeous yellow of the woman's blouse and the pretty gray skirt she'd matched it with, the expensive shoes, and the wide belt on her tiny waist. The woman nibbled at her toast and the man spoke more than she did, but never while chewing. He put down his utensils when he spoke and never took his eyes away from her. Such attentiveness, she thought, couldn't come from a husband. The girls, she knew, had probably already spotted the wedding bands on both of their fingers, but only the girls would know if the bands matched, if the couple had spouses in other places, if their lunch was secret despite its being out in the open.

More customers rang through the door, the bells tinkling their welcome, and the café filled with the clatter of silverware and afternoon greetings and footsteps across the tiled floors. The couple had never raised their voices, even when the café had been empty, but now Arlene could only guess at what they were saying, how the man held the woman's attention, how they talked without ever pausing, without ever glancing away in disinterest. The girls flitted around with coffeepots, dashing back and forth into the kitchen, bringing back turkey sandwiches and chicken-fried steak: They were watching all of this between tasks and they would come up with a story, but it would be the wrong one. They would put it together during the next break time, flipping through *Modern Screen* and finding the picture of that actress and swearing up and down that she was wearing the same earrings if only you looked really close.

They would do so because Bakersfield was that kind of town. Here, people believed whatever story they wanted to believe, even if they made it up, and it had already had its own beginning and its own middle and its own end.

What she wanted to tell the girl waitresses was that life was not anything like those magazines, but she did not want to sound like a bitter woman. She had stories of her own to prove it. But how was she supposed to tell them, when no one bothered to ask her about her life? Especially not lately, since Frederick had left her, and all around her swirled assumptions about the reasons why. When Frederick left her, she was still Mrs. Watson. There was no maiden name to go back to. Not without being able to explain that she was from Oklahoma and he had been from Wisconsin, with no relations in between. She wanted to put down the coffeepot, the slice of apple pie, rest her hand on Priscilla's shoulder, and explain, to tell her real story, as it had happened. To say to all of them, *There's the story you think you know, and there's the one I need to tell you.*

She saw that the couple were beginning to wrap up their meal and she walked over to the table, drawing up the ticket right in front of them, trying to overhear anything they might still be saying, but they were quiet. Arlene ripped the ticket from her pad and set it facedown on the table, but she looked one more time at the woman, as if to invite her once again to admit that she was or wasn't who they all thought. But the woman only stared back at her with a face so shorn of feeling that Arlene did as she had before—she looked away—and her thank-you to the customers came as it did on those days when she was most exhausted, the sunlight orange in the plate-glass windows and the hours too slow, her voice caught in her throat, the very sound that reaffirmed everyone's worst possible imaginings about her. What man, after all, would have stayed with someone who spoke so sharply, in such an unfriendly tone, her head hanging? How could a woman like that possibly be the mother of that radiant man who tended bar at Las Cuatro Copas, the one who made that Mexican shopgirl beam like she did?

"It's her," said Priscilla, watching as the couple exited the café, the man regally holding the door open for the woman. "I think the girls are right, though. That's not her husband."

"That's terrible gossip," said Arlene. "She's a good woman stopping through town is all."

"Did you see the rings? They were different! You can even see it in the magazine!"

"Do you believe everything you read?" asked Arlene. "Now, enough of this nonsense." She tried to look at Priscilla in the same way that the woman had looked at her—cool yet defiant, placid yet standing her ground—but Priscilla only retreated and raised her eyebrows. One of the other girls came into the kitchen, and Priscilla wasted no time in leaning her head in to hers, her voice low and conspiratorial. Like schoolgirls. They made Arlene feel old all over again. She wasn't that old.

She was only forty-seven. She could remember clear as anything being nine years old, sitting out on the front porch at one in the morning with her mother. Way back when Bakersfield wasn't such a big city, back in 1921, their farmhouse on the outskirts of town. One night in August, Arlene had been unable to sleep, even with all the windows and both the front and back doors open for a cross breeze, the summer air stuck in the house. At one in the morning, she rose from her nest of blankets on the living room floor and walked out on the porch, unafraid.

When her mother, awakened by the squeak of the porch door hinges, found her, she came out and sat next to Arlene on the steps. *Why are you out here?* her mother had asked, but she wasn't expecting an answer. *Your brother is going to be the same person you remember when he left. Everything is going to be just like it was. Nothing's changed.*

Arlene walked to the empty booth and set about cleaning up the plates. But things always change, she thought to herself. She wasn't just Mrs. Watson. Her name was Arlene, and she had once had a husband who said her name in the dark, and years ago her older brother had come back from prison to hug her and tell her that she was a sweet little sister. These things didn't change simply because she had no one to tell them to. Arlene wanted to say this to those girls; she could see their faces as she wiped the booth's table clean. She took the ticket and counted the money—the man was a big tipper.

Once upon a time, her mother had told her on the porch, *there was a little girl. She had no shoes and no food and she was walking in the woods. It was very cold, but she saw a little house in the trees and there was a yellow light in the window. She knocked, but no one answered, so she opened the door. The little house was empty. It was very cold and she was hungry and there was a pot with food in it. She could see the steam rising from the pot, so she went to taste it. It was soup and it was delicious.*

She had been nine years old and too old for stories, too old to be resting her head on her mother's lap, yet too young to be sitting alone on the porch at one in the morning. Arlene had listened to her mother's voice and closed her eyes to picture the scene. Her mother was remembering the story terribly, leaving out all the details. Arlene saw herself cold and hungry. Her mother's voice said "woods," but they lived in Bakersfield, California, and there were no woods to be found. There were orchards, but they didn't look like anything in the torn pages of the book of fairy tales from which her mother was trying to remember the story, a dense gathering of trees so gigantic that only the trunks appeared on the page. Arlene knew those trees, having memorized them as she stared at the pages of the fairy-tale book. Orchards had order to them, trees in straight lines in every direction, underbrush cleared out incessantly. *She was cold,* but in the book of fairy tales, that meant snow, which didn't fall in Bakersfield. There was only fog and light rain that lasted for days.

At one point, Arlene had rested her hand on her mother's knee to signal her to stop. When the girl tasted the soup a wolf was supposed to come in, and then a handsome prince to save her, but her mother had the story all wrong in her attempt to re-tell it. Her mother told the story too fast. She did not linger on the darkness of the woods, the yellow eyes hiding in the night. She did not describe the warm glow of the house and how it held a promise of refuge, or the color of the soup, a cue to what kind it might be. Arlene was nine years old, already too old for stories, and had wondered to herself, ever since the day she had stared at the torn pages of the fairy-tale book, why the girl had a beautiful blue-checkered dress but ran barefoot. She wondered why anyone would build a house in such dark woods. She wondered who had been cooking the soup, and why the bright yellow windows were not bathed in steam. She wondered what a handsome prince would want with a girl who had no shoes.

She was a waitress. She was a motel owner. She was a mother. She was an abandoned wife. She served coffee. She had a brother whom she had loved from a great distance, yet never saw again. Her name was Arlene. She served pie. Her name was Mrs. Watson. Her name was Arlene Watson before and during and after. She slid coins off countertops and dropped them into her apron pockets. She wanted to tell this to those girl waitresses to see if they would understand—that she was all of those things, and the town had a story about her and yet the story would never, ever come close to the truth. That she had a story and that it could change and that it was not over and that she was not on the last page. How one day she was happily married, and the next she was forty-seven years old, a thumb on the money in the right pocket of her uniform. *Things change,* she wanted to say. *You don't know anybody's story.*

Arlene thought of the woman and the man and wondered if they were really married, if she was indeed the famous actress, if she was having an affair, what she might be doing in Bakersfield. She thought of the richest women she knew in town and couldn't see any of them wearing a yellow blouse with silk-covered buttons. She lost herself in imagining everything about that woman, even tempted to voice some of her suspicions out loud to the girls, just to see if they might consider her, once again, as one of them. It occurred to Arlene, too, that the woman had stared back because Arlene had indeed discovered something, and it felt like the same stare she gave herself in the early morning hours, just out of bed, when she stared unblinking into the bathroom mirror and wondered how she could go on the way she was, working two jobs and not knowing what was to become of the motel.

The thing was, it was easy to know what troubled her. Her face in the bathroom mirror during the early morning hours said it all. Her face stared back at her, as if waiting for Arlene to ask something of herself.

"You take two tables," she told Priscilla. "I've got a headache." She expected no argument and she thumbed the man's large tip in her apron pocket as she went back into the kitchen, past the large ovens and the walk-in pantry, and opened the door out to the alley to breathe a little.

There was a cabin in a deep, dark forest. Someone built it. Someone chopped down those enormous trees whose tip-tops reached far past the boundaries of the pages in the fairy-tale book. There was more than the book could ever show. Someone cleared brush and sent field mice scurrying. Someone endured mud when the rains came, watched the ground dry out when the sun appeared, judged when it was time to get back to work. Someone took shelter under a canopy of branches as the cabin walls went up. Someone swept out the dust. Someone brought food to the cabin, sewed the red curtains in the windows, hauled in the kitchen table, the large pot to place over the fire. Someone lived in that cabin, and yet the little girl pushed open the door without knocking. Seeing no one there, she made the cabin her own and went right over to the steaming pot, claiming it. Hunger was no excuse. Neither was being lost. There was no rain, only cold, but she had run away from home with no shoes. You had to blame her for being stupid, for running away into a deep, dark forest without a pair of shoes. She must have owned several dresses if she had a beautiful blue one that never managed to get torn or dirty. She was never in any danger at all, really, when you stopped to think about it. Sometimes people are just that lucky. Their story works out. Hunger comes and it's met by a pot of soup. Cold comes and there's a warm cabin with no one in it. A wolf comes with teeth bared, but a handsome prince comes just at the right time to slay it. You never see how. He just does it, and the past gets wiped away. He takes away the girl in the blue dress and gives her shoes and marries her, a happily-ever-after, and no one ever asks about why she ran away from home in the first place.

Four

Around town, she was known as Alicia's daughter—Alicia, that woman who used to work at the café, the woman who left not long after the Bakersfield earthquake in 1952, boarding a bus, it was said, to go back to her ex-husband in Texas, leaving Teresa to raise herself. You remember a woman like that. Teresa had been almost seventeen at the time, just a year away from being a grown woman in the eyes of the law, but she learned quickly that people in Bakersfield had their own ideas about who she was and could be. Alicia's daughter. That poor girl left alone. That girl who lived right above the bowling alley, a green door at street level opening up to a narrow, dark stairwell, the room at the top.

Her mother's name got Teresa the job at the shoe store, not too far away from the café where her mother used to work. Her mother's name kept her from being whistled at too loudly by the small group of Mexican workers who stood on the corner by the grocery store, the ones who had been too drunk to be picked up for work, too shy, too old, all of them watching Alicia's daughter as she closed the green door behind her in the mornings and began her walk to work. Her mother's name kept the attention of the waitresses who still remembered Alicia from her days at the café, the ones who watched her walk by and wondered how a girl so young, supporting herself, could have much to eat in that little room above the bowling alley. Her mother's name, for at least a few years after her mother left, kept Teresa in a strange, collective safety, as if people in town knew they should keep a protective eye on her.

But things change.

People forgot her mother. The name Alicia hardly danced anymore on the tip of anyone's tongue. New waitresses came on board at the café, some from Stockton, some from little places like Delano or Tulare, knowing no one in town. People had other things they wanted to remember, like what the five-and-dime looked like before the TG&Y moved in. People even forgot the earthquake, the terror of the tumbling brick, and the railroad tracks just out of town bent into a slithery S. Teresa herself grew past eighteen, past twenty, and by the time she was twenty-three, not many thought it was unusual that she had her own job and lived in a small room above a bowling alley, her one little window with a dim yellow light glowing at dawn, sometimes the curl of a pale blue curtain fluttering past the open frame.

She felt sometimes, as she closed the green door behind her and began her walk to work, that people had forgotten all about her, that they'd not only forgotten about her mother but about how her mother had left and why, and once they'd forgotten that story, Teresa would also disappear, like a figure into fog.

She liked thinking of herself this way, as if it were one of those winter mornings when the Bakersfield streets clutched the fog deep into the asphalt and her own steps dissolved into all that white without a sound. What could people possibly know about her now? What could they say, when the years had eroded their concern and she walked with near anonymity along the streets of Bakersfield, no one wondering anymore just how she was going to take care of herself?

You have, her mother had said to her, *a very good head on your shoulders.*

She could do, she realized, whatever she wanted. She was twenty-three and her own woman.

When had this idea bloomed in front of her? On one of her walks to work, no doubt, all those mornings, five days a week, sometimes six, when she came down the narrow stairwell in whatever weather. Every day the same thing, the Mexican workers on the corner, the initial whistles, then the fervent admonishment from one of the men to settle down: Cheno remembered her mother. He used to buy a work lunch when Teresa's mother sold bean tacos or ham tortas during the summer months, Teresa collecting the coins. He knew they should treat her respectfully. Cheno, who was a little shorter than the rest of the men, neither the oldest nor the youngest in the group, the one without tattoos, who knew how to keep his white shirts white, who endured the taunts from the men when he rushed to defend her. She knew he was standing a little apart from the men, as if to guard her as she walked along the block, as if waiting for her to come back. But of course, by the time she returned home from work at the shoe store, the men on the corner had already dispersed, some because they'd been picked up as extra hands in the fields, the rest because the police had chased them away for drinking beer, even if it was in a paper bag.

She thought of Cheno at lunchtime, when she took some of her hour to walk over to Stewart's Appliances. The store, with its shiny radios and washers and sewing machines, was only for people with money. So Teresa stood outside the enormous store with its plate-glass windows reaching all the way to the sidewalk—built brand new and shatterproof after the earthquake—and watched the television sets, six of them playing without any sound. All six sets played a lunch-hour newscast, sometimes flashing pictures of the stark white regal domes and pillars of Washington, D.C., or some other faraway place, and Teresa patiently waited until it was over and the 12:30 musical show came on. A woman sang. Always a different woman, but always the same posture, the same stance—hips angled over to the side and arms straight down, her voice slowly rising to a crescendo Teresa could never hear from behind the window. She stood watching these soundless lunchtime concerts, and anyone watching her knew that she was dreaming beyond the desolation of Bakersfield's dusty streets to a stage like the ones those women occupied, or to the theaters glimpsed by the audience when the cameras cut away to the interior: tiny round tables and elegant glasses, rows and rows of plush-looking seats. Velvet stage curtains and a spotlight like a tender moon, the full force of all manner of musical instruments, and men at the ready to play them: guitars, pianos, drums feathered gently, saxophones held to the lips with almost unbearable hesitation. Teresa daydreamed as the women sang because she couldn't hear them through the glass. But she knew it would be over when the women's arms finally reached outward to the camera, as if pleading, as if asking a lover back or sending him away, their mouths rounding out to release a last note held so impossibly long that Teresa thought she heard a glimmer of it through the thick plate-glass windows.

On afternoons in the dark quiet of the shoe store's stockroom, she'd think of her mother boarding a bus and she would think of the hills south of Bakersfield and the pictures she saw of Los Angeles. Her mother had been heading to Texas, but Los Angeles would be the first city she would see, and Teresa wondered if her mother would be moved by the city's pageantry and decide not to continue. *You'll understand one day,* her mother had said, *when you fall in love.* Her mother's words stayed with her for a long time, like the embraces of the chanteuses on her afternoon viewings, full of longing and never letting go. They filled Teresa with both hope and sadness: She understood, as she slid box after box onto the dusty shelves of the storeroom, that she had to fall in love first before she could be any of the women with the open arms. She understood, too, that this same hope and sadness led her imagination to put her mother back on the bus for the long hours to Texas, what she thought would be the hot, dusty sands of the Southwest before the bus stopped with a hiss and the door swung open for her mother's release. Her mother with the open arms and someone there to receive them.

So when Cheno appeared one evening, the only person on the corner as she arrived home from work, she waited for him by the green door to her little room above the bowling alley. They stood there talking for a bit in Spanish and she asked him if he had worked that day. He said yes; she could tell that he was lying but she appreciated the effort that he had made, his plain white T-shirt tucked inside his pants, a faint hint of bleach carrying in the air, mixing with the Lucky Tiger oil he used to slick back his hair. Even the way he had hesitated in crossing the street charmed her a bit: tentative, looking at her as if awaiting a sign from a distant star.

They talked for no more than fifteen minutes, her hand on her purse even though there was nothing to guard except her key, and when he parted, Teresa knew he would be back the next day. She let herself in and climbed the stairs, immediately going to the window to peek out, just in time to see his form make its way down the street and finally turn a corner, heading west, walking all that way to the side of town where men lived too many to a house.

The next day, when the Mexican men on the corner watched her emerge, the usual taunts began. "¡Ay, mi amor!" "¿Adónde vas con mi corazón?" She walked on but cast a quick glance to see if Cheno was in the group, attempting to quiet them. He didn't catch her looking for him, but she was heartened by the uninterrupted catcalling, certain that Cheno had done no bragging of his own. That evening he appeared at the corner with two lukewarm bottles of soda, which he uncapped against each other, and this was the start of his small, edible gifts: candy bars and fresh peaches and cans of Kern's nectar and dried apricots and shelled walnuts packed into an empty Gerber baby-food jar.

They'd eat these treats sitting on the curb in front of the green door leading up to her apartment, mostly in the early part of the week. The closer the days got to Friday, the busier the bowling alley became in the evening, and Cheno withdrew, as if he didn't want to be seen by anyone. She liked this about him, as if their short evenings were a secret between them, despite meeting out in the open. As the days passed, her affection for him grew, the way his gentle fingers carefully handed over his latest gift, not wanting to touch and offend her, his round eyes taking her in like light. She began to notice mornings when he wasn't at the corner at all, the catcalls uninterrupted, and these disappearances alarmed her at first, until she figured out that he was wheedling himself into more work. She left the curtains open one night so that the dawn light would wake her as she lay in her bed under the window. She hoisted herself up on her elbows to peer down, and sure enough, there was Cheno in the hushed violet of five in the morning with a few other hard workers, ready to go, and not ten minutes later, he climbed into a farmer's truck and was whisked away, his head turning toward her apartment and his gaze steady on her window.

It wasn't love. She knew that. But she liked the attention, wishing to herself that maybe time would transform her feelings into the kind of longing her mother had displayed, the longing that drove her back to Texas. When they had lived together, her mother had played old blues records with women singing the way only women could about love, love gone right, love gone wrong. Sixteen records that her mother cared for rigorously, searching for scratches, easing them back into their paper sleeves, bringing them out only when the mood struck.

Pull out the one with the red slip, her mother had told her one time. They sat on the bed, right underneath the window to catch the evening breeze, two glasses of water with ice long since melted. *Man from Abilene,* her mother had told her, a sad song, and the way her mother requested it, Teresa had known that sad music was something that you should listen to alone.

The crackle of the needle brought the easy strum of a guitar and a harmonica. Her mother hummed along but sighed and gave the singer space for her lament, not interrupting. The singer moaned, cursing Abilene, a whole story of pain that could have been avoided if she had ignored the deep brown eyes she still managed to sing about. The guitar strummed along, one beat after the other, a monotony, but easy to tap your heel to. *Put it on again,* her mother had said.

Outside, just like the morning Cheno rode off with his love-struck ambition, the street held violet and their rented room had darkened enough for Teresa to watch her mother close her eyes and listen to the song. Her mother had played that song hundreds of times, yet as their room darkened, Teresa made out the burn of her mother's sorrow only by the sound of the song, the way she hummed a little louder when the lyrics matched her own life.

All of her mother's records were like that in some respect, some speck of phrasing, some line or two that could draw out the *mmm* from her throat in confirmation. *Again,* her mother had said with a sigh, the violet of evening seeping into their room.

Teresa didn't want to be like that. She watched the street corner begin to buzz with the approach of the Mexican workers and thought of Cheno. She could never be like her mother for Cheno. Love could not be a heavy darkness. It could not be violet light in a window, fading. She wanted love to be like the open arms of the women singers in the display windows of Stewart's Appliances, all receiving and nothing ever lost.

It felt decisive, this feeling about how to control her own heart, and she set out to work as she always did, the catcalling and the stale dustiness of the storeroom and the glow of the TV sets in the store window all coming as familiar as ever. Days passed, and when Cheno didn't appear, she began to miss his presence, the street bare of anyone when she approached her apartment in the early evenings. More and more days passed and she began to wonder if Cheno had left for more lucrative work up near Fresno, a silent room in her heart wondering if, in fact, another woman had caught his attention.

Whatever filled her about Cheno's absence was neither anger nor loneliness nor regret, but she could not identify it, could not place words against what it was. Teresa sank at the possibility that the dark space inside her would spark into one of those emotions, a tiny match struck in the dark—how easy it would be to become her mother upstairs in that room with its single bed under the window and the empty kitchen table with two chairs.

When Cheno finally did appear, her relief came as a surprise. Even from two blocks down the street, she could tell it was him, the gleam of his white T-shirt, his small frame waiting patiently by her door. He'd returned after all, and even if it hadn't been love that stirred within her, she sighed at the release of the mysterious grip within, grateful to have Cheno back.

The closer she walked to him, the more she could tell he was holding something, a large, bulky object, and when she crossed the last street and neared the apartment, she could finally make out the rounded curves of a small guitar that Cheno held in his arms.

"Un regalito," he said, handing her the gift.

She took the guitar. "Where have you been?" she asked him in Spanish.

"Al norte," he said. "Pueblitos." He'd gone way north of Bakersfield, staying in small labor camps, following whatever crops he could and saving his dollars, and she knew his motivation without needing him to declare it. Even after presenting her with the guitar, Cheno kept his hand on the fret board, holding his fingers there as he told her about the day he'd seen her in front of a store window and how, after she'd walked away, he'd gone to see what she'd been watching. The show had ended, but he asked someone, who told him the young girl always watched the afternoon variety show to see the singers.

"But a guitar?" Teresa asked. "I don't know how to play."

"I'll teach you," Cheno said, his voice so sincere and small that Teresa could do nothing but smile and clutch the guitar to her chest, embracing it, before dipping her hand into her purse and extracting the key. She had no worries about Cheno doing anything untoward. Even as he followed, his steps feathered up, as if he were hardly there, as if he were floating, as if he had been down on the street corner as he'd always been, alighting with his small boots in the air and coming right through the open window of her small room, the light blue curtains parting for him.

How long did this go on? It had been late summer when he'd given her the guitar, her apartment still orange in the late evening. Cheno left whenever daylight started to go. She kept the guitar in the closet on his urging, covering it with a light cloth, and whenever he returned, he'd turn the instrument round and round in his hands, checking for cracks before handing it to her. He taught her a few chords and they'd share whatever treat he'd brought her—lemon drops or dried, sugared mango—as he listened to her practice, his patience infinite. She got to thinking, at times when she watched him demonstrate a chord she was finding difficult, that he was the only person who'd been in the apartment besides her mother, yet her mother's dark presence was long gone, and as the months drifted into fall and sundown came earlier and earlier, she finally made it clear to Cheno that it was okay for him to stay a few minutes longer after she turned on the bare bulb in the center of the room.

You'll understand one day, her mother had said at the bus station. *When you find a man of your own, you'll know why you'll run toward him.*

Teresa served him dinner once—just once—a small bowl of beans with onions and two corn tortillas, which Cheno ate with relish, his thanks never ending. He refused a second plate. It was getting dark, he told her, and it was best he got home. She watched him from the window as he went down the street, hurrying, and part of her wondered if his secrecy was meant to protect her, to keep anyone from seeing a strange man close the green door at the base of the stairwell.

She knew he was going to ask her to marry him. Not soon, but one day. What she felt for him was affection, not love:

she liked the thrill of pulling him closer and closer, then the slight edge of relief when their guitar lessons were over for the night. There were days he stayed away and Teresa knew he'd gone back up into the northern parts of the Valley to make money, but even so, she didn't want to leave the safety of her single room. It was hers and she was a twenty-three-year-old woman walking down the street and she was no longer Alicia's daughter.

"Do you sing?" he asked her in Spanish.

She was about to say yes but realized that the songs she hummed to herself were all in English. She didn't know how he would take this. "Sometimes."

"Would you sing me something?" He took the guitar and, surprisingly, began to strum something she recognized, a Patsy Cline song. She laughed and shook her head, refusing, but he kept playing the chords over and over until finally she complied, the song she knew so well from the dim glow of the radio, which she left on at night to lull her to sleep. She sang "Walkin' After Midnight," casting her eyes over at the open window, remembering her mother and how the room had to be quiet when her records played, the only sound the pain in those women's voices.

"Que lindo," Cheno said when they finished.

"Gracias," she answered, and she was not surprised when Cheno reached over and touched her hand. She could feel the thin plastic of the guitar pick between his fingers, his touch light and unsure.

"We should sing together," he told her in Spanish.

"What song?"

"No," he said. "I mean in public. At El Molino Rojo."

"Why there?"

"So we can earn some money," he answered. He kept his hand on hers, very light, as he would have done if he'd emerged from the secret shadow where he stood watching her in front of Stewart's Appliances, reading her desires in the shows flickering across the screen, touching her shoulder. He was asking her for complicated reasons, Teresa knew—to fulfill her dreaming, yes, but also to make their work a joint effort, not just his own sweat in the field.

"But how?" she asked.

Someone on the corner had urged him to go audition at El Molino Rojo, where the bar owner let people sing for tips. Cheno's plan was to go there on Tuesday afternoon, her day off from the shoe store, and meet her there once he finished whatever fieldwork he'd managed to get that day. She knew what side of town he was talking about, the avenue over on the west. Over there was El Molino Rojo. The Wild Horse. The Bluebird. The clientele went to the bars where they could pronounce the names. The signs in English glowed amber at night, an electric necklace of shimmering bulbs, some of them buzzing neon: the Fiddle, and Rosie's with the namesake petals blooming in light. The Mexicans went to the cantinas with names beautiful and full of promise, even if the buildings were tucked away in the dark, no neon to speak of. El Club Diamante. El Paraíso. Teresa's mother had spoken of cantinas in Texas with names that sounded just as regal. El Presidente. Las Angelinas. Saturday night the one night of the week for elegance, for the dress made from expensive-looking fabric purchased at the TG&Y.

Such places! Such names! Why hadn't the idea occurred to Teresa first, all those afternoons dreaming in front of Stewart's, as if her mother had never given her stories about the cantinas up and down the state, over there near San Antonio, near Temple. La Lupita, La Conga. Even the little towns past the onion fields and the sweet potatoes had cantinas. Beeville, Kenedy, Mathis, and on to Corpus Christi. El Siete de Copas. El Espejo. El Gato Negro. El Peek-a-boo.

There was no reason, really, to go against Cheno. Women sang in bars like that. People watched them and listened. Old blues songs or honky-tonk or country or ranchera ballads, laments in the native tongue of the clientele. So she agreed to meet in front of El Molino Rojo the following Tuesday afternoon, her day off work, and when the day arrived, she pressed her white blouse and her denim skirt and smoothed her hair in the bathroom mirror. Then she picked up her small guitar with no case and no strap and went down the stairs, emerging into the white heat of the afternoon, the men on the corner too drunk by this time of day to notice her.

At the far end of Union Avenue, El Molino Rojo stood near an intersection, tucked in a bit from the road. The building was unassuming, a small shack with dark windows and a flat roof, rough wood siding, tall yellowed weeds growing along the edges of a gravel driveway, the bare signage scripted badly by someone's shaky hand. Teresa walked across the gravel parking lot, even though the door to the building was shut, and ducked under the faint shade of the roof's overhang. The street was quiet.

She put her hand against the dark windows, trying to see

inside, and felt foolish about knocking. Cheno was nowhere in sight. Teresa rested the guitar against the wall and fanned herself. Her stomach gurgled with hunger and she wondered how long she should wait before turning around and walking back home.

A black Ford truck slowed and pulled into the gravel lot across the street. The driver shut off the engine, and the dust from the driveway settled as he stepped down and made his way to the front door. He was tall—Teresa could tell that even from across the street—and he rattled the heavy chains that served as a lock to the cantina before pulling the door open, its metal growling against the cement. He stepped inside without shutting the door behind him.

The street went quiet again. Teresa looked at the building's sign: LAS CUATRO COPAS. Its door stood gaping open, as if it had swallowed the man forever. She could hear the ticks of his Ford pickup as its engine settled and cooled.

The man emerged from the dark interior. He was looking at her, finally raising his hand to shade his eyes as if it might help him see. Teresa remained motionless, embarrassed now that she was out in the open. The man stepped outside and began walking toward her, his boots crunching on the gravel drive-way, not looking before he crossed the street.

Halfway across the parking lot of El Molino Rojo, he called out to her, "You waiting for Ed?"

Teresa didn't know whether to shake her head no or speak to him, but he crossed the rest of the parking lot in no time at all. He glanced down at her guitar. "You waiting for Eduardo?"

"The manager, yes," she said.

"That's Ed, then." His eyes remained fixed on the guitar. "You'll be waiting for a while. He doesn't come in until much later on Tuesdays. Nobody drinks this early on a Tuesday."

"Oh," she said, trying not to pause, as if to suggest that Ed had been expecting her. "I figured I would just wait for him."

"You singing for him?" He didn't give her a chance to answer. "He's got too many people already. Everybody and their mother thinks they can sing a song."

She straightened a little when he said that, and the man took her posture for apprehension.

"I didn't mean it like that," he said. "It's just that . . . well, I can't tell you how many people show up and ask Ed to let them sing for tips."

"That's what I had planned," she said, shaking her head in embarrassment.

"What's your name?" he asked. This time, there was kindness in his voice, as if he recognized that he had been too brusque. His voice wasn't just kind but apologetic. She looked up at him, his brown hair still singed with a light color on top from the summer days, his nose slightly sunburned.

"Teresa," she said.

"You're Alicia's girl, aren't you?" He shielded his brown eyes with his hand against the sun, but he studied her as intently as he had studied her guitar. "Yeah, you are—you look a lot like her in some ways. Around the eyes, I mean."

"You knew my mother?"

"She worked with my mama at the café. Everybody knew your mama. She was a real nice lady. Did you know Mrs. Watson? Arlene Watson?"

She shook her head.

"I'm her son. Dan." He stuck his hand out and she reached to shake it. Even though it was hot out, his hand felt cool to the touch, her hand tiny in his palm.

"It's good to meet you," she said. She tried to keep her hand light in his, not knowing when to let go.

"She around anymore? She didn't pass, did she?"

"No. She had to go back to Texas," Teresa said. "Family." She spoke with a nervous hesitation, and Dan Watson seemed to catch the waver in her voice. She could tell that he already knew her whole story, but his face didn't betray it.

He smiled at her instead and pointed at the guitar, and the way he smiled eased everything. "You want to sing for me?" he asked her. He leaned over and picked up the guitar with great care, holding it out to her. In his hands, the guitar looked like a toy, small against his frame.

Teresa shook her head. "I should be heading home."

"Come on, now," Dan Watson encouraged her. "Just one little song." When she shook her head again, laughing, he stepped closer, nearly placing the guitar in her arms. "You can sing at the Copas if you're any good."

He held the guitar out to her. She thought of the women on the television sets at Stewart's Appliances, the women not just singing anymore but speaking to her somehow, letting loose with their admonishments: this was why they held out their arms at the end of every song, they would tell her, because someone like him might reach right back.

"You want to go across the street? Have some water and rest a little while I'm setting up?" he asked. He had a hint of a singer in his voice, the way it rose and fell, yet still nestled in sincerity. He placed the guitar in her arms, and his brown eyes held hers for a moment before he backed away and began walking toward Las Cuatro Copas.

"Come on," he called out, half turning, as he walked. After that, Dan Watson didn't turn around again. He was tall, his back wide, his brown hair thick against the sun. The sound of boot steps on the gravel slowly faded as she watched him disappear inside the building.

She stared across the street at the dark opening of Las Cuatro Copas. Where was Cheno? Her hands clutched the guitar and she heard her feet against the gravel, and she found herself at the threshold of the bar, her eyes slowly adjusting to the darkness inside.

"That water's for you," Dan's voice called out to her, but she couldn't see him, her eyes still not acclimated. She stepped in, making out a long bar against the lefthand side, with stools padded in royal blue velvet. She reached for the glass, grateful to be out of the heat, the ice water stinging her lips. She looked up at a ceiling fan whirring, an old swamp cooler rattling high in the corner above the bar.

His boots sounded against the floor and he emerged from the other side of the cantina with a plate in his hand, the swinging door to a kitchen padded red with a diamond-shaped peep window. "I'm not much of a cook, but I can make sandwiches," Dan said. "You looked hungry."

"You didn't have to bother," Teresa said, but her stomach gurgled at the sight of the plate, and she held her hand over her stomach as if Dan could have heard it.

He stepped behind the bar and set the plate down, spying her empty glass and refilling it, even tossing the old ice into the sink and giving her fresh cubes. He pointed to the sandwiches as he poured himself a beer. "Go ahead and eat. It's just ham and butter. That's all the kitchen had back there that I knew what to do with."

She took one of the sandwiches. The butter gave it an unusual taste, but Teresa didn't complain, even though the bread was thick enough to catch in her throat. She had to swallow water with every bite.

"Aren't you going to join me?" she asked.

"Oh, no," he begged off. "You eat as much as you want; it's all for you. But you'll have to sing for your supper, of course. That's the only requirement."

She smiled at him as she took a bite, nodding her head in agreement. "So there's a little kitchen back there?"

"Just basics. Nothing fancy. We cook a few things and bring them out to people with their beers. See the tables?" He motioned. "We're a little less rowdy than Ed's place. More dancing over there, more coming and going." Dan tipped a thumb back to his mouth as if taking a drink. "Too much sauce over there sometimes. Gets out of hand. Very . . . worldly, if you know what I mean."

"Worldly?"

"Things go on in places like that," he said, sighing.

"Right across the street?"

"You'd be surprised what's right across the street, no matter where you go." He slid the plate closer to her. "Go on. It's all for you. I already told you you're singing for your supper."

She took another sandwich and he busied himself behind the bar, washing glasses and counting beer bottles. She tried to eat as slowly as she could, and the thick, heavy bread helped, but before she knew it, her hunger had won over and the sandwich was gone. Almost as soon as Dan Watson saw the empty plate, he said, "So how about that song?"

From her seat at the bar, she could see outside to El Molino Rojo, across the street, but Cheno wasn't there. She took a drink, the water having warmed some in the dissipating heat of the cantina, so it wasn't too cold for her throat. The song she had practiced was one she had tried to recall from her mother's record playing, a simple set of repeated chords, but now the idea of singing in front of someone besides Cheno felt ridiculous. "I'd be terrible," she said. "I don't know what I was thinking."

"Come on, now," Dan said. "I gave you a sandwich."

She laughed. Cheno was still nowhere on the street. "I suppose," she said, a bit defeated, yet somehow relieved that her number wasn't going to be a real audition. She smiled at Dan's good nature and bent down for her guitar, adjusting herself on the blue velvet stool and looking down at the strings in preparation.

"No, no," he said. "Not there." Dan pointed to the center of the cantina. "Over there." He stepped from behind the bar and grabbed another blue velvet stool, handling it as lightly as he had the guitar, bringing it to the center of the room and setting it gently on the dusty floor. "Right there," he called, then retreated toward the kitchen. She didn't have time to imagine how the cantina might look at night, full of people, the sound of boots on the wood drowned out by song and laughter and chatter. A honey-colored spotlight came on from above. "Go on," Dan called, but she couldn't see him anywhere. "I can hear you."

She laughed nervously but took her place, her stomach sinking and her hands beginning to shake. So this was what it was like to perform, to call out while everyone was hanging on your words. Her knees felt watery and wooden at the same time. None of it felt right: her posture, the honey light, her throat clearing but her voice sounding reserved, her fingers too jittery to focus. But she held them on the strings just as Cheno had shown her, and took a deep breath, imagining herself on the television sets at Stewart's Appliances, remembering that the singers and the fiddle players and the horn section always faced the camera. So Teresa looked up, as if she were facing an audience herself. Ahead of her, on the opposite wall, a long horizon of mirror stretched from one end of the wall to the other. There she was, with her denim skirt and her white blouse, and the light coming down like hot honey. She was too far away from the mirror to see herself clearly—her features, her face, the way her eyes must have looked, confused and full of apprehension—but she was close enough to see that she would never be a distant figure to anyone in that cantina. She would be close enough to the patrons that the songs would mean something if she sang them the way she did in the quiet of her rented room above the bowling alley, and she could focus on the image of herself in the mirror if she didn't want to look in their eyes, just the way she did with Dan Watson outside in the heat of the day, his eyes squinting to conceal what he was really seeing.

Seeing herself in the mirror, she suddenly felt calm, the idea of her singing not so ludicrous.

She began, her fingers already on the strings, and she strummed the first notes, watching herself in the mirror as the opening words came out of her mouth:

I had a man
In Abilene
Man of my dreams
But lowdown mean.

She was mesmerized by the sight of her hands caressing the guitar, her fingers moving in time over in that mirror and keeping up, but it lasted only a moment—Teresa felt the next notes getting away from her, and she stopped singing but kept playing. She had to bend her head to watch the strings, to concentrate, to remember the words and keep time.

Prettiest eyes
I ever seen
In Abilene.

The song had escaped her: her voice was clear, but her guitar playing lagged behind badly and she had to strum the chords between lines a few times to catch up. As she sang, her mind wandered to the ease of those women on the television sets, all of their energy focused just on the emotion of a song she couldn't even hear through the heavy plate glass. They had it easy, she thought, struggling, her knees growing heavy from the guitar. She watched the strings, watched her fingers, but when she neared the last verse, she stopped playing the guitar and just hummed, looking up at herself in the mirror, focused entirely on the way she always wished she could see herself: poised, controlled, assured, brave. Not lonely, not frightened behind two locked doors, not longing for her mother, not longing for Cheno to be a different man, not opening her eyes to yet another morning of a life with no one in it, no money, her heart too heavy with worry. Her own image in the mirror showed this to her with such nakedness that she found herself singing as loudly as she could, and she surprised herself at how much lament she was able to muster, as if to make up for her uninspired performance, as if to sing out to herself in the mirror. She wanted to watch herself, but she found her eyes closing, her head rising up some as if the last notes knew on their own that they could slide out of the arch of her throat.

Dan clapped from his dark spot, emerging into her honey light, smiling so widely that Teresa could only believe he was doing so to make her feel better. She looked down at the guitar as if it were to blame, and as Dan's boots sounded closer against the wooden floor, she felt foolish and sorry for herself. That was what she had seen in the mirror—her own deep need, all of her longing apparent—but nothing about it could be appealing. She thought of Cheno watching her in front of Stewart's Appliances and had to look at the floor.

"Don't put your head down," Dan admonished her. "That was great." Then he reached over slowly and tipped her chin up, one finger and tenderly. He didn't keep it there, but Teresa wished he had, just as in the movie advertisement she'd seen outside the Fox Theater downtown, a woman with watery eyes looking up at a man, his hand on her cheek.

"Thank you," she said, but she couldn't look at him, at his brown eyes, nor back down at the guitar strings, so she went back to herself, over in the horizon of mirror, looked at herself as Dan Watson stood over her, his wide back, and the honey light coming down.

"You're a good singer," he said. "A sad voice sells a lot of beers."

"Sad songs are good?"

"Oh, yes. Especially here. If you want to dance, you go over to Ed's place. Get drunk and cry? Right here."

Dan reached over for the guitar and she gently released it to him. Confidently, he started up the song again, this time with a bold, strong rhythm and none of her hesitation. She watched his fingers along the fret board, astounded. They were strong hands, agile, one dancing along the arm of the guitar with instinct, the other striding along with equal, easy fervor. "Your guitar playing needs a little work, though."

She laughed, but he kept playing, smiling back at her. He wasn't watching his fingers—he didn't need to. Dan Watson was looking right at her, his brown eyes wide and inviting. "Sing," he said. "Come on."

What the song sounded like, now, was what she remembered from her days with her mother, and she didn't need to close her eyes to make the words arrive. They came on their own, and because Dan Watson was now blocking her view of herself in the mirror, she looked at him as she sang. She kept her voice low, but the feeling was there, the sorrow. But now she was beginning to understand that such sorrow had a different shading to it, that it could lift into something else if she permitted herself to sink exactly into the whirl of Dan Watson's brown eyes, the eyes the song warned about.

Teresa kept her voice low and the two of them carried through the song with an easy harmony that actually made her smile when they finished.

"I knew what song you were trying to sing," Dan said. "My mama used to listen to it a lot."

"So did mine," Teresa said. "It was one of her favorites."

"You changed the words around."

"I didn't remember them," she admitted. "Or I remembered hearing it differently."

"You start inventing words, that's true," Dan said, handing back the guitar. "Playing is harder than it looks. You practice a lot?"

"Not enough. I don't know that much about how to play."

"Who taught you? Your daddy?"

She couldn't find the best answer, thinking of Cheno outside, wondering if he was searching up and down the street for her.

"You have a nice voice, though," he said, reassuring her.

He stood smiling at her, and when Teresa couldn't think of how to respond, she laughed nervously. He laughed with her but wouldn't say anything more to help her out of the fluttering tension in her hands, her stomach, her throat. She looked down at the guitar and picked at one of the strings.

Dan reached over and moved her left hand to the fret board, positioning her fingers. "Right there. Bend this finger. Firm as can be." Satisfied with her grip, he eased right behind her with one solid step and cast his arm over her shoulder. Not touching her, but close enough for Teresa to feel the soft fabric of his shirt. He helped her play the briefest of notes, just the beginning of something, unsaid and unsung and sad-sounding enough to warrant feeling that way, and then stopped.

Outside, through the open door, a vehicle sounded across the gravel, slowing down. The vehicle stopped and they could hear a door open and close. "That's Ed," he said. "Across the street."

He stepped away from her, and Teresa rose from the stool to look out the door, but all she saw was the vehicle—another Ford truck—and Cheno nowhere in sight.

"Sing for me," Dan said.

"That's the only song I know."

"No," he said, shaking his head. "I mean, sing for me, not Ed."

That's how it begins, the women on the television told her. *You have to open your arms wide first.*

"I'll play guitar," Dan said. "Or someone else will. All you have to do is sing."

Across the street, the door to Ed's bar stood wide open, but it wasn't a place she wanted to enter anymore.

"I can't pay you," said Dan quickly. "You can keep any tips, though."

Had Cheno come and gone? She thought of what he might say when she presented this situation to him, but what made her dismiss him was the spark of her mother's voice, the need when she sang along with those records, and what bloomed in Teresa was something close to forgiveness. Of course her mother would've boarded the bus to go back to Texas.

"Okay," Teresa said, and nodded. "I'll sing for you." Then she froze. "You don't mean tonight, do you?"

"No, no. Practice first. Practice as much as you want. In here, if you like. In the afternoons when I do the cleaning, so you won't feel nervous."

He made his way to the front door, picking up his keys from the top of the bar. "Unless you're going to help me sweep up, maybe I should take you home right now before the drunks come in."

"I can walk," Teresa said. The old feeling came back: she wasn't just worried about Cheno seeing her in Dan's truck, but about the people in town, how a ride through the afternoon streets with the windows rolled down was far different from Cheno's careful, tiptoeing courtship.

"It's not a problem," Dan said. "Come on."

Seven years ago, when her mother had announced that money was too hard and that they would both board a Greyhound to Texas, where Teresa's father lived, Teresa had said, *I'm not going with you.* Saying that had been like singing a song: opening her mouth and letting the sound crack through. She knew, even then, that Texas was not for her, that her mother wanted to go to the place where the records took her, the violet dark where Teresa's father lived. She had said no, the static of the record turntable going round and round, and she couldn't see her mother's face when she said it.

Dan locked Las Cuatro Copas and made his way to the black Ford pickup truck, opening the door and holding it for her. Teresa looked across the street at the other bar, hoping to catch a

glimpse of Ed or even Cheno, some opportunity to stop herself
from her own falling, but the building only yawned back with
its open door, Dan standing, waiting, his tall, wide-shouldered
posture.

"Come on," said Dan. "What are you waiting for?"

It's your life, her mother's silhouette had said, after a long silence between them, in the violet dark of their little room. *You
do what you want.*

Five

She had known, since it was Bakersfield, not to expect anything fancy, but as the driver took them through the center of the city, it became clear to the Actress that all she was getting was a room, plain and simple. She didn't need anything more, really, though she imagined there were people in the industry who begrudged everything. The driver stopped the car at a building that wasn't more than four stories or so, flat at the top and made of brick, and they got out. She opened the door on her own, the driver rushing to her side, but she let him know implicitly that he needn't be at her beck and call. They walked together through the plain glass doors of the lobby— no bellhops, no concierge, but more important, no Director. She had somewhat expected him to be waiting in the hallway lined with striped wallpaper that served as the lobby, sitting at one of the two tidy love seats and examining the fresh flowers set on a long table: the hotel was small, but the effort of small-town pride came through. It was only nine thirty in the morning, and the meeting wasn't set until ten. She asked at the front desk if anyone from Los Angeles had checked in, but the clerk told her no.

"Are you expecting someone?" the clerk asked.

"A fellow traveler," she answered, aware that the Director might try to shield himself from scrutiny.

Her room was ready, and the driver accompanied her to the top floor in the tiny elevator, her overnight bag in his hand. At her door, he scurried inside her room and placed the bag on her bed so quickly that she barely had time to open her purse for a tip. "No bother, ma'am," he told her. "The studio asks that I not take tips. I'll be with you the entire trip anyway." He gave her a slight nod and made to exit. "I'll be waiting in the car after you freshen up. I'll have the front desk ring you if the Director shows up."

He closed the door behind him, leaving her alone in the room. Nothing fancy, as she had suspected: a tidy double bed, a nightstand with a lamp and a radio, and a desk tucked in the corner. Enough space for the Los Angeles and San Francisco oilmen to come to town, make their deals, and get some rest. The air felt a little trapped and still, as if no one had actually been in the room, not even to turn down the sheets and check the towels. But this didn't surprise her—if it had been her job to go from unused room to unused room, she wouldn't bother with these tasks either; she would kick off her shoes instead and listen to the radio, the minutes of each work morning slowly passing by.

That's what she was thinking of—what it would be like to be a cleaning woman in a small hotel in an inconsequential city, the daily humdrum of that kind of life. Her mind circled around that scenario as she unzipped her overnight bag and set aside her belongings, giving tomorrow's blouse a quick snap before putting it on a hanger. She imagined the uniform and the soft shoes, pushing a cart along the narrow corridor she'd just walked along, the quiet red carpet, and the discreet closet at the end where the cart would be hidden away overnight. There was more, she knew, as she emptied her toiletries and set them around the bathroom sink, confident no one would come in to clean: say, for example, the awkward moment when a hotel maid politely knocked on the door and, hearing no one, came in even though the guest was sleeping. Or the curiosity around a stranger's suitcase sitting like a diary in the corner of a room, the temptation to unzip it and rummage around. Or the toiletries kit left in the bathroom, the inside pocket holding a vial of pills that spoke of nerves, of insomnia, of depression, of a lingering sexual disease.

In her movie script, she had read the description of her character: secretary. She had read the setting: Phoenix. At a leisurely lunch, the Director had told her how he'd already sent a set crew to Arizona to find young women working as secretaries, interviewing them to see how much they made a year, how they dressed, what they ate for lunch, where they ate it, if they had husbands or lived alone or with girlfriends, what their apartments looked like, how they furnished them.

For what? she had asked, because the scenes that took place in the office and the woman's apartment were brief.

To get it right, the Director had told her, taking a long sip of wine. *I want it to look like a girl's apartment, you see. Right down to the cheap dresser.*

It was a pity, she had thought as she looked over her salad, that she hadn't been invited along, if only to witness how the set decorators found these young women and how they engaged them in conversations that, frankly, could slip into the nakedly personal without much effort. She didn't let on to the Director that she'd been disappointed about missing such a trip. That wasn't the purpose, she knew. Listening to him explain the purpose of a set—the information conveyed by the atmosphere of the walls, the correct wallpaper, the furniture just so—made her feel that her own concerns about who a secretary might really be had no place at their lunch table.

The Actress knew the answer even now, staring at the clock in her hotel room, five minutes to ten. Smoothing her dress and looking at herself one more time in the mirror, she saw her own incomparable face, the size of her head, her eyes set apart, her breasts, her hair. A singularity. There was no one else like her, for better or worse, and she had been picked for the part for the sum of these attributes, and maybe nothing more. The Actress gathered her pocketbook and headed down to the lobby. She knew the answer, and it would take only a hotel maid to appear in the hallway to confirm it, two women passing silently by each other without knowing a single bit of the other's history: it was a costume, she realized, not a complexity, a job for the character to have, not a way to explore how she'd come to that point, a single woman in Arizona, of all places.

Down at the lobby, the Director was still not there. "Has there been a call?" she asked the clerk. "We were expecting another party from Los Angeles."

The clerk shook his head. "Early morning traffic from Los

Angeles can be very heavy some days," he said in a voice that was meant, she thought, to allay some concern. She turned to sit on one of the love seats and looked out through the plain glass doors at the street's light traffic. She waited as patiently as she could for twenty minutes, at which point she rose and walked to the glass doors, not exiting but peering out of them as if the Director were only moments down the sidewalk.

Inside the sedan, her driver sat engrossed in a newspaper, its pages folded compact and neat so that he could hold it in one hand, flipping it when the column ran out of text. With no traffic and not enough people on the sidewalks to disturb his reading, he carried on without once glancing at her. The paper was thick, probably the *Los Angeles Times* and not the local, and she wondered what he might be reading—an article about the troubling political changes in Cuba, the sports section, the satellites being sent up into space one after the other. She didn't want to interrupt him, but there was nothing else to do, and across the way was a café with large plate-glass windows through which she could see if a car that looked like it belonged in Los Angeles came along the avenue.

As soon as she opened the hotel door, the driver glimpsed the bit of motion, set his paper down, and rushed to her side of the car. "Oh, I've got nowhere to go," she told him. "I was just going to go across the street for a bite to eat."

"I suppose you don't need to be driven there," he said, laughing. "I'll be here if you need me."

"Actually," she said, this time looking away from him and over at the café, "why not come along and keep me company?"

He hesitated, as if contemplating what it might look like if he left his post, but the Actress waited through his caution, letting her face go blank, no anticipation, no hint of persuasion, though she knew it wouldn't be a prudent thing for him to do, the way the studio frowned upon anything beyond the call of obligation and service. But it was her invitation, her decision to bring him along, and she wanted to open her mouth and assure him, *It's okay,* but instead she stood and waited for his inevitable yes, wondering how she looked to him, her face impossible to read.

They did not enter arm in arm, but the two men seated at the front counter didn't seem to notice. The hostess locked eyes with them for just enough time that the Actress wondered if she'd been recognized, but the driver quickly snapped the hostess to attention, asking to be seated. The hostess gave them a booth, the Actress with her back to the sidewalk because she knew the driver would be more attentive to the car they were expecting. The café smelled thick of disinfectant, a moist, greasy feel to the air, but not unpleasant once she recognized it—it was the smell of any diner in Los Angeles, and soon enough, she knew, would come the smell of coffee and eggs and frying bacon and their masking familiarity. She studied the menu, feeling eyes on her. She should have worn dark glasses, but she'd long dismissed the idea, a pair of shades feeling, to her, like a prop inviting attention. Perhaps the eyes were taking in the driver, in his crisp white shirt and slacks unlike any of the other men in the place, with their scuffed boots and jeans.

When the hostess took their order, the Actress tensed at her scrutiny and did her best to divert the attention to the driver, the man at the table, as if she deferred to him in everything. He may not have understood the role she had imposed on him, but the way he cheerfully ordered a full breakfast plate did the trick. The driver looked over at her sheepishly when he placed his order. She'd had an orange juice and a croissant to tide her over, but she realized that he had had nothing, and even after arriving at the hotel, he was still at the call of duty, waiting in case she came out to be driven somewhere. A break was some time off, perhaps when he knew the Director would be taking up a good chunk of her afternoon.

"I should have realized you hadn't any time for a decent breakfast," she told him. "We should have come down here as soon as I'd checked into the room."

"Ma'am, my responsibility isn't over until your Director takes you away. And even then, it would be the professional thing to stay around in case you need something. A bite to eat if you don't like what's on set. Or some aspirin from the drugstore." He spoke with a light, cheerful clip in his voice, but it was still deep and masculine, his face lined here and there on the forehead, someone who raised his eyes a lot and smiled handsomely.

"You mentioned your wife on the drive over. How long have you been married, if you don't mind my asking?"

"Not very long. Three years," he answered.

"You have children?"

"No, not yet," said the driver, but he didn't add anything more, and in that lack of continuation, the Actress held her eyes on his, not wanting to look away and reveal her immediate wonder about his wife: if she could bear children, if she came from a religious family, if she was ill, if she had been the right woman to marry.

"Someday," he offered, the single word still feeble despite the confidence in his deep voice, hard lined and rigid straight like the horizon of his shoulders. "It must be tough for you as a mother to be on these shoots."

"It is. I'm thinking more and more that I won't be doing it very much longer. I'd rather be with my children."

He blushed a little. "I didn't even ask if you had children. I mean . . . well . . . I knew . . . I've read about you in the magazines, so . . ."

She laughed. "Oh, I understand. But those are just publicity stories," she said. "Some easy facts. You could never get a true understanding of anyone from those accounts."

"Of course not," said the driver. "But you do come across as a very nice lady. People like you in this town. In Hollywood, I mean."

The early lunch crowd trickled in, yet the sidewalks remained relatively bare otherwise. The waitress who brought their plates wasn't the same one as before—she was much younger and prepared to chat, staring at the Actress as if she were a puzzle that needed solving, but the hostess who seated them dismissed her quickly. The café began to gather its noise, the waitresses striding by with coffeepots and checks in hand, sliding coins into the pockets of their uniforms. The Actress buttered her toast, a meager little breakfast, aware of the stares on her despite all the activity. The driver splotched some ketchup on his eggs and tore into the bacon with a determined but measured hunger: he still held his knife and fork carefully, as if remembering he was eating with a lady.

"Do you mind if I ask you about the film you're making?"

Without the benefit of a full plate of food to help her deflect the question, she paused for a moment and pursed her lips. "I'm under orders not to, I'm afraid to say," she said apologetically.

"I won't say a word if you don't," the driver responded, no food in his mouth, everything politely chewed and swallowed, a man with thick dark hair and manners and laugh lines on his forehead, as if maybe he were living without any anxieties, any second thoughts.

She took a bite of toast, thinking. She stole a glance at one of the customers near the windows, a woman, catching her in the act of being nosy, how they were making everything of her Los Angeles attire, the driver's crisp white shirt and how strong his back looked to them, the full plate of food, his hearty appetite.

"Well," she began, "I suppose it wouldn't hurt, since you've been so kind."

He smiled and took a bite of eggs, prepared to listen.

"I play a woman—a secretary—who is carrying on a romance with a man who owns a little hardware store here in California. Not Bakersfield necessarily, more in the north, just a little town where you can remain anonymous if you want to, live a life without anybody paying much attention, if you color inside the lines. This secretary, she lives in Phoenix, though, and she doesn't have a way to be with this man whom she loves so very much."

"What was the man doing in Phoenix? How did they meet?"

"Good question. I don't know. A salesman, I suspect, however

clichéd that is. But I suppose it doesn't matter. It's at the beginning of the movie, so the scenario is just something you accept.
Don't you agree? If a picture starts, and there's a man and a
woman, and they say they're in love, you believe them. Right?
At least, that's how I'm approaching it." She didn't believe that,
but she appreciated the driver's question, tinged as it was with
the same urge she had for answers to the lives of characters,
even if the answers weren't very important. "In any case, her
lover goes back to California, just about calling off their affair
because the situation has become impossible and unbearable.
They live in different states and the man has an ex-wife who
is taking all of his store profits for alimony. What kind of life
could they live together?

"That very afternoon, at the office where she works, her boss
makes an extraordinary sale to a wealthy man and asks her
to deposit the money in the bank. She agrees and then asks
to leave work early because she has a headache, but instead of
going to the bank, she goes home, packs a suitcase, and decides
to drive to California."

"She steals the money?"

"Yes, all of it..."

"A bad girl. I don't think my wife and I have ever seen you
play one before." He looked surprised, the rise in his voice suggesting that he disapproved, so much so that the Actress debated if she should continue.

"It's a challenge, I admit. To play against type."

"I'll say. Aren't you afraid people will have a negative reaction to you playing that kind of woman? A thief?"

"She's more than a thief..."

"An adulterer. I forgot about that part."

"It's a complex moral dilemma. That's the way I like to think about it." She took a sip of her tea, a sharply bitter black tea with a strange taste. She set down the cup. "I also believe that audiences are sophisticated and wise enough to separate you from the role you play."

"To a degree," said the driver. "But if it's the wrong part . . . I mean, if people remember you so strongly in that role, people may not ever forget you in it. Do you remember that picture from a few years ago? I don't remember the name . . . It was about the little girl who envied things so much she killed people to get them."

"*The Bad Seed.* Interesting play, to say the least. I saw it in New York, but I never saw the film."

"Yes, that's the title. Last year, I bought a television set for my wife, and we like to watch those theater shows, the playhouse specials. You know the ones? And whenever that little girl shows up, no matter what the role, my wife makes me change the station. She really hates that little girl!"

The Actress laughed. "That little girl has the benefit of getting older. I'll bet your wife doesn't remember her name."

"She probably doesn't. Just the blond pigtails. Innocent little girl otherwise. But you . . . ," he said. "You'll look the same, movie to movie. Don't you worry about that?"

He went back to his food, waiting for her to answer, and she didn't quite know how. She understood what he was getting at, the thorny reaction of the public, its fickle nature, but even in a generous view of her career, she was hardly Elizabeth Taylor or Audrey Hepburn or Grace Kelly or any of those gilded actresses with something to protect when it came to script choices. She wasn't the same, she wanted to tell him, tapping the sticky café table with a hard nail to prove her point. She wasn't going to look the same from movie to movie—she was going to age.

"I hope I didn't upset you," he said.

"No, no. I'm just thinking about what you said. It's a serious question. I take your opinion very seriously."

"I'm sure it's a good role. And he's a very famous director. I'm sure you'll do fine," the driver said. He was stammering his assurances. When she didn't respond, he began eating again, slowly, without looking up at her, and she felt a bit of sympathy for him. He was clearly embarrassed by his questioning, unaware that it might have been insensitive, but perceptive enough to note that it wasn't any of his business, that the role was, after all, a choice. Something she could have turned down if she felt strongly enough about how the public would perceive her. He was handsome, but he wasn't stupid.

The Actress took a sip of the sharp tea and absently tore off another piece of toast. The driver's plate had been piled high, and even with a hearty appetite and their new silence, he wasn't anywhere near half-finished. She contemplated what she'd told him thus far about the film and how he had reacted, realizing that she'd left out all the nuance. The two scenes in a brassiere. Her lover appearing shirtless on-screen. The interrogation by a policeman and her successful evasion of the law. How she had been written to exit the picture. She'd given him hardly any of the story, but he'd latched on to morals. He would go back to Los Angeles and—he would certainly tell his wife—he'd say he brought around that Actress to star in a picture featuring her as a thief and an adulterer. Not a secretary. Not a woman in love. It was her own fault if he came away with that impression. She'd been asked to tell the story and had told it in only one way.

He put down his fork. "Ma'am, I apologize. I can tell by the look on your face that I've upset you."

"No, no. You didn't," she reassured him.

"But you're so quiet all of a sudden . . ."

She reached over and rested her hand on his, the right hand, the one he would need to use to lift the fork, but she only thought of that after she pressed into the warmth of his skin, the eyes of the hostess at the café's counter burrowing into her gesture, as if she knew that wives didn't touch their husbands exactly that way.

"Really," she said, smiling. "You've given me plenty to think about. You're extremely thoughtful to ask me those questions. Sometimes we forget what it's like to be someone in the audience, how they might perceive things."

For a moment, the Actress thought the driver might take his other hand and clasp hers—he was looking down, not at his plate exactly, and not at her hand, just down in a posture that suggested a deep regret that didn't befit their conversation. He looked ashamed and she felt for him and she didn't want to take her hand away from his, not even to allow him to pick up his fork again and eat away their silence.

With his thumb, her hand still on his, he traced a light, downward feather of a touch, just once. Then his hand went still once again, and it became clear to her that she was the one who had to let go.

"We think the world of you," the driver said, and it was he who cautiously took his hand away. "My wife and I."

They ate the rest of their meal in silence, and though the driver kept his eyes on his plate and never glanced at the avenue, she knew that the Director and the crew had not yet arrived. The clock above the counter read eleven thirty and already a full lunch crowd was there. When the check came, she tried her best to insist on paying for her toast and black tea, but the driver refused, and she spared him the indignity of having the eyes of the café watch him take her money as if his own wallet were not enough.

He held the door open for her, and before she stepped outside, before she lost the humid, thick smell of the café and before she was greeted by the dusty odor of the sidewalks, she caught the briefest hint of his aftershave.

She sighed. "I guess we just keep waiting. It's closing in on noon, and the scene we were supposed to shoot today takes place in the morning."

He looked up at the October sky. "Can anyone tell the difference?"

"Some people can. The shadows. The way light plays on the face. Especially now in autumn. The sun is a little lower in the sky. You can tell what time it is just by looking outside, can't you? Roughly?"

"I suppose you're right," the driver said, putting his hands in his pockets.

"You know, I really can't imagine that I'm going to need you to drive me anywhere for the rest of the day. Why don't you check into your room?"

"I'm not staying at this hotel, ma'am. Me and the crew find places over off the highway, where the truckers stay."

She knew what those places were, the side motels she'd seen along Highway 99 leading into Bakersfield, work trucks parked patiently in their gravel lots while the drivers rested for the night, a long row of identical doors, identical rooms, meager by comparison to her own hotel room across the street, simple as it was. The Sleep-Tite Motel. The Knight and Day. The Stardust. Their neon signs off during the daytime, but as the highway approached the outer edges of Bakersfield, they sprang up closer to each other, and she pictured how they might look to a weary driver, a cluster of safety in the darkness, and such a long day of driving that sleep would come with alarming ease, no matter the endless traffic droning on through the night, just outside the door.

He led them across the avenue, and she peered down the road one more time but knew the afternoon was now lost. She wondered briefly—then stopped herself—if there might have been an accident, and by wishing the thought away, she removed it as a possibility. They were running late was all, and when the Director finally arrived, he'd prepare everyone with a new schedule for the brief, decidedly private shoot. It was just the beginning of work on the film—the preliminary stages—and the hard work and the curiosity from the public was yet to come.

"Well, I suppose there's not much else to do but go up and take a nap."

"Yes, ma'am."

"You should probably go on ahead and check into your room. Save yourself some time. I honestly won't need you this afternoon."

"Only if you're sure, ma'am. I can wait here until the Director arrives."

"No, no," she begged off, and started toward the hotel door, and he moved with her, then ahead, in order to open it for her.

"Very well," he said. "I'll call the front desk on the hour, so if you change your mind, let them know. I'll drive right back."

She smiled in thanks and was about to step into the lobby. "Driver," she called out. "Listen, I feel terrible. I've never even asked you for your name."

"Carter," he said, returning her smile, and he bowed his head a little.

"Thank you, Carter, for everything this morning," the Actress said. She stepped into the lobby, knowing he wasn't going to follow, but disappointed still when his footsteps failed to sound behind her. The desk clerk nodded at her in greeting and also in silent affirmation that he had heard nothing yet from the missing guest, the lobby completely empty of any sound, any movement, and she walked to the tiny elevator and waited in the quiet, while the desk clerk turned a single page of newspaper to sink into his afternoon reading.

No one in the carpeted hallway, no maid's service cart to inspect and memorize in passing, no maid with a downturned look of exhaustion. No one, she began to believe, on the entire floor. The Actress entered her room and took off her shoes, sitting on the bed to massage her feet. It had been a long morning, and she'd been up so early for the driver to bring her all the way here, only to wait.

A nap would come easy in this silence. She walked over to the door to double-check its lock, and once she was done, she removed her skirt, her blouse, and the constriction of her bra and lay on the bed. She closed her eyes, replaying the conversation she'd had with the driver, regretful of how she had described the role. Could she have told it to him in another way? Would it have mattered? It had been the only moment, really, when the driver had been anything but cordial, kind, respectful, the look that had washed over his face when he realized she would be doing something wrong in this picture. She opened her eyes and rested a hand on her naked breast and sighed. That look on his face. And over a bundle of stolen money. What if she mentioned the detail of the lunchtime tryst in a little hotel room like this one? *I saw the script call for the opening shot to be this woman rolling around luxuriously with her lover. She isn't wearing a blouse and you can see the hair on his massive chest.* That soft feather downturn of his thumb tip and whether or not he would have done that.

Carter. It could have been, she realized, either a first or a last name.

Because she was alone and no maid was ever going to come down the hallway, and because the door was locked even though she was certain the other rooms had gone unoccupied, the Actress rose from her bed and walked to the mirror and stood in front of it. She stood absolutely still in self-examination, her reflection cutting off at the waist, so all that was visible to her was her naked torso, her face, her eyes. She had all afternoon, she knew, to stand in front of that mirror in scrutiny, the way empty time manages to hand you nothing but doubt. She had to be convinced it was acceptable to play that first scene in a brassiere, even if the whole theater would have believed a man and a woman being inescapably in love simply because the screen story said so. A whole theater of men looking at her in a brassiere, a whole darkness wanting. She drew her eyes down to her breasts, beautiful and round. Never had she caught the Director looking at them—always at her eyes. Still, she kept thinking of those other actresses, their entrances, their slow-motion kisses, their gowns, their mystery and allure from their first glimpses onward. Maybe it wasn't much of a role; maybe those other actresses had been approached and had wisely turned it down. The Actress stepped back from the mirror, as far as she could before she reached the opposite wall. She took in the entire image of herself, the doubt as thick as the quiet in the hotel. But she would show them. She would show herself. You don't just put on a maid's costume and dust the rooms. You have to know the uncertainty of interaction with guests who couldn't care less, the ache in your back from bending down to make beds. The Actress was going to play more than a woman who steals money. She was going to play a woman in love, who does something wrong for the sake of it. Her hand on the driver's a gesture at understanding how it felt to do something illicit, how it felt to draw someone into sin. A woman who was a secretary in a dusty Arizona city. A woman who had a sister who loved her and would later look for her. A woman with a moral choice, who makes the right one in the end, no matter that the story itself could have cared less what she did or did not do, her little car moving from Phoenix and on westward, the drive so long you'd think she was going to drive off the end of the earth, in a love so deep she was willing to disappear into it without a lingering trace.

Six

From the moment Teresa boarded the pickup, she expected to see Cheno coming up the street, and every figure walking along threatened to be him, only to end up being no one at all that she knew. Dan Watson drove with such leisure that she wondered if he didn't already suspect that she'd been waiting for someone, and she did her best not to appear nervous, her hands tucked underneath her knees, the guitar resting between them. When they rounded the corner toward her street, she seized at the thought of Cheno waiting at the door, even though it was something he'd never done. The street was bare. The way her pulse raced and eased when she discovered this alarmed her. She was doing nothing wrong.

Dan Watson kept the truck running after Teresa pointed to the green door. "Right there?" he asked.

"Yes," she answered. "I live above the bowling alley."

He peered up at the window, the blue curtains hanging. "I didn't know that was up there."

She opened the door. "Well, thank you for the ride."

"You working tomorrow?"

"I am. Today was my day off." She stepped out of the truck and held the door.

"Can I pick you up for lunch?"

She pressed the guitar against her. "Well . . ."

"Noon? Is that when Carson lets you off?"

"How do you know I work at the shoe store?" she asked, both astonished and a bit amused.

"Small town," he said. "How 'bout it?"

Something told her that she was supposed to hesitate, but the words bubbled on their own. "I'd like that," she answered.

"Okay, then," he said. "Noon it is." He reached over the bench seat to close the passenger door. "I'll see you then."

Teresa scurried up the steps in the dark hallway, and for the remainder of the afternoon she lay on her bed and watched the room tilt from deep yellow to the orange of the west. She kept expecting to hear Cheno's voice from the street, her windows open to break the heat, but by now she realized he'd been kept at whatever fieldwork he'd been given for the day. Still, she wanted to hear his call, his tiny knock at the foot of the stairs, but as evening came, she thought more and more about Dan Watson and found herself not wanting to see Cheno at all. She let the violet come as her mother had done in the past and didn't turn on the light. From below, she thought, maybe Cheno would see the dark window and think she'd gone to bed early.

She ate in the dark—a simple dinner of leftover beans heated gently on the stove, and two tortillas. She drew a glass of water from the tap. She thought of Dan sitting down at a table in a large white house, plates and plates of food, and the silhouettes of his family gathering round.

When even the violet light disappeared, Teresa showered to cool herself off before sleep. She stretched her little radio closer to the edge of her bed, its cord extended as far as possible, and turned on the dial. The face of the radio glowed amber, now the only light in the room. She lay on the bed and listened, irritated by the announcer, but then grateful for his information: he told her the names of the songs and the singers singing them, and each time one caught her attention, Teresa closed her eyes and listened hard. She tried to memorize the words, even though they floated past too quickly, and caught lines here and there when they repeated as a chorus. Men cooed together sweetly, standing behind the one singer as if to help in his pleading: that was how men sang. Songs of pleading and promises, tomorrows, wedding days, and love eternal. All of them in voices so high pitched that they sounded nothing like the men downstairs: they sounded regal, silky, like looking at cigarette smoke but not having to smell it.

Downstairs, she thought she heard the faintest of knocks, and she reached over to turn down the radio. She heard it again, a timid one-two, and then the pause that meant Cheno was waiting, looking up at her window, and wondering if he should knock again.

She wanted to raise herself up on her elbows and look down from the window. He'd come all that way. It was so late. She could feel him waiting. But on the radio, a new song started. It was a man. And all evening, whenever a man sang, she pictured

Dan Watson. If a woman sang, Teresa imagined herself. Even the backup singers had a role, two or three Dan Watsons behind her in complete harmony if the song required it, or sometimes two or three versions of herself, in different-colored cowgirl skirts, with Dan playing a guitar and all three versions of herself reaching out to him from the single microphone.

Downstairs, she could hear Cheno's footsteps give in to his indecision. Her heart ached for him a bit as she pictured him walking the streets of Bakersfield, dark now, and she lay back down on the bed. Sleep wasn't going to come tonight, not the way her eyes closed and she saw visions of the pickup truck or the ham-and-butter sandwich Dan had served her or his hands pressing her fingers on the fret board. She reached over and turned up the radio, listening awhile before finally noticing the balance struck by the DJ: sometimes a song would be low and quiet, the love lost, but then a girl group would come up next and chirp like birds about the wonders of a simple smile. They sang as if none of them had ever sat in a dark room with their mothers. They sang as if they always answered the faintest knock at the door from someone too timid to admit his own love. They had voices like sunny mornings, full of a hope so assured it wasn't really hope anymore.

Could she ever sing like that? She wasn't sure. But Teresa couldn't manage the songs of desperation either. She had nothing within her that could match that complete loss of hope. She was alone and she was lonely, but she was not her mother. Could she make it up, imagine that pain? Which song could her mother sing, which one could most truthfully speak to what she carried inside? She wondered how much of one's life mattered in giving a song conviction, how much could be heard by a stranger who looked at you knowingly. She closed her eyes and imagined herself singing with Dan. They would have to be, she told herself, happy songs. Unless she thought of Cheno. Then it would be different.

The hours passed and Teresa drifted into sleep, too heavy into it to reach over and turn off the radio. She woke when a ballad came on, so hushed and strange, as if Cheno himself had stolen into the room and started singing for her. Her sleep confused her, this voice and the words being sung. The voice registered defeat and weariness and surrender. She woke enough to picture Cheno and then a whole company of boys she had seen around Bakersfield. The dull, gangly son of the shoe store owner; the two high school boys who rode their bicycles together in the mornings, both of them rail-skinny and sporting thick black glasses. That voice could come out of any one of them in complete sincerity, she thought, but her mind floated back to Cheno.

"That was Ricky Nelson's hit from last year, 'Lonesome Town,'" said the announcer at the end of the song, and Teresa thought to reach over and turn off the dial. But she had loved this warm weight brought on by music as she tried to sleep, and she closed her eyes, hoping for another moment like it. She drifted in and out of sleep, at one point hearing a different announcer, with a voice barely a whisper, saying that it was nearly two in the morning, and for a brief moment she dreamed of rising to look out the window to see what Bakersfield would look like at that hour, who else the announcers were keeping awake, the stars above the dark city. That was her at the

window, naked, and the men at the corner grocery store looking up but not whistling, as if seeing her like that at night was a
gift they knew they shouldn't question, just behold.

Morning trucks began coming around four o'clock, only a
single engine now and then, but enough to wake her and open
her eyes to the sky lightening to indigo. The radio kept playing. By the fourth truck she peered out at the corner to look
for Cheno, rubbing the sleep out of her eyes, and sure enough,
she saw him haggling with a driver, his white T-shirt almost
glowing in the dawn light. When she saw him jump into the
bed of the truck, she watched the brake lights disappear down
the road, his head turning back to look at her window, and she
wondered if he saw her. She rose soon after and took her time
preparing her blouse and skirt for work, making coffee and two
slices of toast. She bathed again to get rid of the night's sweat,
dried her hair, and put it up in a bun. It was only seven, still two
hours before she had to be at work, but she gathered her purse
and descended to the street.

At the foot of her door, as soon as she opened it to the morning, she spotted the little jar. She bent down to pick it up. A
Gerber baby-food jar, filled to its brim with toasted pumpkin
seeds. She held it in her hand for a moment before placing it
in her purse along with her apartment key. It was hardly any
weight at all, but she could feel the little jar like a stone in her
purse, almost pulsing with Cheno's long patience at her door
the previous night. This wasn't right, the way she was behav-
ing, and sooner or later, Teresa knew, she would have to say
something to Cheno. But what, exactly, when all she knew

was the uncertain fluttering deep in her own throat at every thought of Dan Watson.

She headed to the shoe store in a roundabout way, wondering if she was in love. She lingered by a sale display of laundry detergent, nail polish, and floor wax at the drugstore and found herself dreaming of using them in a large, beautiful home with Dan's pickup parked in the driveway. Across the street, she was surprised to see the barber shop not only open but busy— she could see the men waiting in chairs, reading the morning paper, and could even hear the soft buzz of a radio report. Married men, all of them, she suspected, maybe even what Dan would turn into later on, and when she thought this, she spied one of the men looking up from his newspaper, his eyes lingering on her.

She walked away from his gaze and went to the record shop down the street. She studied the album covers pasted up against the windows, Elvis Presley and Peggy Lee and Frank Sinatra, the black discs hanging down from the ceiling on fishline, each of them with colorful labels that Teresa regarded as if they were jewels. The logos, the rich colors, even the company names: Chess, Atlantic, Peacock, Imperial, Sun, Decca, Mercury, Capitol, Cadence. Since no one was on the street, Teresa said the names aloud, wanting to hear how grand they sounded, each with its own singularity and suggestion, and she stood there dreaming about which life she'd rather have: one with Dan and the pickup in the driveway, the other where she could arrive at one of those studios in an elegant car, the microphone waiting.

To ask for both, she thought to herself, was greedy beyond words. She thought of Cheno, if he daydreamed while yanking nectarines from the branches, what he asked the sky for.

In the bottom of the corner display, she noticed the name Ricky on one of the album covers. She had to lean down to look at it, at him. There he was, a black-and-white picture, but she guessed that his hair was brown, rich and deep, and he looked back at her with eyes she could not guess the color of. Maybe blue. Maybe green. But the long lashes! Casting shadows almost, and she studied the rest of his face—his lean nose, the faint bit of stubble, his eyebrows leaning in to each other, the way his left eye seemed to signal a different kind of feeling: the regret she had heard in his voice last night. That was the eye she focused on, as if she could feel his longing, as if she could fall in love with it and alleviate it. Didn't Cheno have it, too? And yet why couldn't she fall in love with him? She put her hand on her purse, feeling the small weight of the jar of pumpkin seeds. Ricky's bottom lip jutted out thick and full, the upper one much thinner, his mouth holding in a perfect line, capturing who he was—a singer—and how everything that mattered about him centered on the moment he opened that mouth.

For hurt to matter, she thought, you had to be beautiful. She thought of Cheno's small frame scrambling into the bed of the pickup truck. She thought of Dan Watson, how even he lacked the long lashes and strange eyes of Ricky Nelson. She thought of her father, whom she had never met, and wondered how handsome he was to lure her mother all the way to Texas.

Cars rumbled by more frequently now, so Teresa made her way to the shoe store, waiting outside the doors. Mr. Carson had not yet arrived, nor had Candy, her co-worker. Sunlight warmed the sidewalk. She could feel the heat in her shoes. Mr. Carson was always early, so by the time his Oldsmobile approached the store, she knew it was probably eight thirty.

He parked fastidiously, poking his fat head from the car window to peer down at the painted lines on the asphalt. He locked the car with his key and approached, a paper cup of coffee in one hand, a small white bag in the other.

"You," he said, searching for the key to the store. "What are you doing here so early?"

He was genuinely surprised, Teresa could tell—there wasn't a hint of malice in his voice. "Just a few minutes is all," she replied.

"Well, don't expect to get off early," he said, holding the door open for her. The giant round oak clock read twenty minutes to nine, and without needing to be told, Teresa walked quietly to the back of the store, through the archway blocked off with a thick beige curtain, and to the aisles and aisles of boots and sandals.

She and Candy had a small worktable near the back door, all of the inventory ledgers neatly stacked, the single rolling chair waiting. The floor was cement, and all day came the echo of their clicking shoes as they searched for a requested pair from the stock shelf, or the scrape of the ladder being pulled into place. A second phone could be accessed from their desk, its bell to be answered by the third ring if Mr. Carson failed to get it at the front of the store. A large floor fan, for the moment, sat turned off. The room, Teresa realized, was actually quiet for once. She listened to the silence, the clock's tick, the slight creak from one of the shelves settling, everything so faint she could hear the shuffle of Mr. Carson's newspaper out front as he turned the page, then the quiet again, as if he were thinking.

She knew Candy had arrived when Mr. Carson's deep-throated but friendly voice greeted her, a little muffled because he'd been caught with his mouth full. The two exchanged morning banter with an unforced pleasantry, something he rarely did with Teresa.

It was not yet nine. Candy finally parted the thick beige curtain and walked across to their worktable. She smiled wanly at Teresa but did not say good morning, passing a few minutes shuffling papers, and when the clock finally struck nine, she turned to Teresa with a clipboard and a stack of salmon-colored index cards.

"Will you do the inventory of the shoes on those racks over there?" Candy pointed to the far wall. "We're getting a shipment sometime next week, so Mr. Carson is planning to put those ones on sale."

"Of course," Teresa replied, taking the clipboard and then going over to the worktable for a sharpened pencil. It would be slow and tedious work, checking each of the boxes, noting the condition of each pair of shoes—some of them had lost their shine after being tried on so many times—but it would keep Teresa occupied until lunchtime.

Fifteen minutes passed in quiet. They were intolerable, lunchtime forever off. This is what it was to be in love, Teresa thought, her heart possessing complete control, allowing her neither rest nor distraction, relentless and constant as a star. She looked at the clock yet again, the long hours until noon.

She was on the ladder when she heard Candy's footsteps approaching, and she looked down in time to see her appear at the front of the aisle, arms crossed.

"You were here so early today," Candy said. It had not been a question, but she looked up at Teresa with a measure of genuine curiosity. But there was something else, too, Teresa saw, a vague shadow of suspicion.

"I was up at dawn," she told Candy. "I didn't sleep very well last night, so I ended up leaving my apartment very early this morning."

"You have a record player?" Candy asked.

"Well . . . no, I don't," Teresa answered, but now her admission felt almost like a defeat, like when the salesman at Stewart's Appliances had approached her the one time she dared step inside, the way he had asked her, "Are you interested in purchasing this television, miss?"

"I have one," Candy said. "Pricey."

"I'd imagine so."

Candy moved fully into the aisle now, her arms still crossed in front of her.

"You going to buy one someday?"

She looked down at Candy, unsure of how to answer. "Maybe I'll save for one."

"They're expensive, you know. Did you know you have to buy needles all the time? Or else they scratch your records if they're not sharp enough."

"What do you mean, needles?"

"For the record player," Candy answered, her mouth opening a little in surprise when Teresa looked back at her blankly. "The arm on the record player," she explained. "It has a tiny needle that fits exactly—exactly—into the groove of the record."

"I see," said Teresa. They remained looking at each other, Teresa on top of the ladder and Candy at the bottom, arms still folded, the silence drawing longer, more awkward. She realized then that maybe Candy had seen her in front of the record store.

"All of that—the needles and the records—starts to add up. That's a lot of money for a salesgirl," said Candy.

"Who bought yours?" Teresa asked.

Candy's arms tightened in their fold. "A boy I've been seeing."

"That's generous of him."

"He's a sweetheart," said Candy.

Though she was on the ladder and above Candy, Teresa felt vulnerable and intimidated, as if it were not Candy at the bottom of the ladder but Mr. Carson's awkward teenage son, trying to look up her skirt. Candy's banter was odd—she rarely spoke to Teresa except to give orders.

"I saw you," Candy finally said. "In front of the record shop. I was on my way to get a couple of doughnuts for me and Mr. Carson and I saw you standing out by the window."

How long? she wanted to ask Candy. Teresa pictured her standing across the street the entire time, silently watching, with hardly anyone else around to notice either of them. She imagined seeing herself as Candy had, looking at a still figure admiring the glacial turns of the records hanging from fishline, the shimmer of the window, and how easy it was to guess what she desired.

But there was nothing—was there?—in Candy making note of her standing in front of the shop. Teresa looked down at the clipboard and the salmon-colored index cards as if they might give her an idea of what to say. Candy, though, spoke first.

"You stand in front of store windows a lot," she said.

Teresa swallowed. "I like to watch the variety shows at lunch," she said calmly.

"The singers," said Candy. "I didn't know you sang."

"Well, I don't—"

But Candy interrupted. "I saw you yesterday, too. Riding in Dan Watson's truck." She looked up at Teresa, and the tone in her voice was unmistakable: accusatory, yet not mean spirited, a flat statement that dared to be denied, as if she were confronting Teresa with an empty cashbox, wordless, yet with the facts in hand, a fact that needed to be explained.

"He was taking me home," Teresa said cautiously, the words feeling too deliberate. She knew immediately that she would not be able to say either too little or too much.

Candy already had a story in her head, standing there in her pleated purple skirt, a thin gold bracelet shimmering on her wrist, her blue blouse with a stitched pattern on the collar, a sheer pink scarf knotted at the side of her long throat. She shopped at department stores rather than make her own clothes from Simplicity patterns from TG&Y—that much Teresa could tell just by looking at her, though in truth she knew nothing about Candy. Candy gave her things to do, instructed her as if she were the boss when in fact they were hired to perform the same tasks. A pretty girl who shopped at department stores, who owned a record player, was being courted by a sweet boy, and yet somehow still wanted more and could not hide it.

Teresa knew she shouldn't say any more, but she wanted Candy to know and not know at the same time: "He plays guitar and he's teaching me," Teresa said, and the moment she said it, she realized for the first time that maybe her own life could be an existence that others could dream about. That everyone, at one time or another, stood near a window and looked out, imagining a life that was not their own. "How do you know him?" she asked, because she wanted to ask the questions now, not just answer them.

"Everyone knows Dan Watson. Just like everyone knows Mr. Carson. Just like everyone knows everyone here."

"No one knows me."

"I know you," said Candy, but both of them knew it wasn't so. All she knew was that her name was Teresa and that she stood outside store windows for a long time and that the most handsome man in Bakersfield had opened the door to his pickup truck to give her a ride home.

Mr. Carson's heavy, lopsided footsteps sounded at the entrance to the storage room, and that finally broke Candy away from the aisle. She eased back toward the desk as if she had never carried on a conversation with Teresa, simply going on with the business of the morning, and though Teresa could not see Mr. Carson, she knew Candy's demeanor had worked. "Oh, there you are," she heard Mr. Carson say, and then he began discussing a matter for the front desk.

Teresa went back to her inventory. *I know you,* she kept hearing as she counted out pairs of sandals she remembered having ordered a year ago. *I know about you,* she imagined Candy saying, and there it was—just the additional word, the single key and the lock turning for a door that revealed everything about Teresa in glaring light: her father gone, her mother following, money scarce, the men below her window whistling. *I know all about you,* she tried, this time her own voice saying it, repeating it, as she counted out white shoes favored by the nurses at the hospitals, tasseled flats in elderly beige, pink canvas sneakers, dancing shoes with glittery straps and heels as thin as expensive vases. *I know, I know, I know,* as she wrote her counts onto the salmon-colored index cards, the morning passing along torturously and Candy not saying another word to her.

I know. But Candy didn't. Here was a pair of shoes like Candy's, a modest pump, the heel barely off the ground, dark brown and plain, no intricate patterning. Teresa glanced at the price on the box and wondered how much Mr. Carson would reduce it—a single pair left, but maybe she could afford it if it went on sale. Women like Candy purchased such shoes throughout the year, the price not too high for them. Candy had a record player and could walk into that record shop and buy every Ricky Nelson song she desired, a different version of his beautiful face on the sleeve any time she wanted.

Teresa continued her inventory but noted more and more shoes she wanted to buy for herself, taking a single index card and jotting down the styles she would pay attention to later. She held them up for inspection: spectator shoes, stack heels, plain Mary Janes and ballerina flats, espadrilles and pumps. All of these for Candy, all of them purchased for her by the sweetheart boy she was seeing. The noon hour crawled closer, and the closer it came, the more she thought of Dan, the things she could have with him, and she felt an impatience that she didn't have them already. When she came across a single pair of cowboy boots—chocolate, the left one scratched badly at both the tip and the heel, a ring of delicate brown roses etched around the mouth—she took one out of the box and held it up as if it could be broken. How unfair of Candy to want more than she already had. Teresa glanced at the shoe size and knew it would fit, then checked the other one to make sure they were a matching pair, as she was supposed to. There was only one pair of the boots left, meaning Mr. Carson had sold them well, but this box had been stuck near the top of the rack, its cover a little dusty from waiting.

Teresa held still, listening for Candy before she even knew what she was actually doing. The floor fan had not yet been turned on and she waited for some kind of signal of Candy's presence in the silence of the storeroom—a shuffle of paper, Candy's shoes against the cement floor, a cough against the dust in the air, but the place remained quiet. The longer the silence went on, the more Teresa hesitated, and she strained for the bells of the front door or voices or the telephone. Nothing came. The longer she waited, she knew, the greater the chance she would never have the boots.

She stepped off the ladder with the boot box in her hand and walked down the aisle, listening. Candy was not at the desk. Teresa stopped momentarily and listened once more. The clock read twenty minutes to noon; the lunch hour was finally arriving. She bent down to get one of the large paper bags with sturdy twine loops, CARSON's printed on both sides. Briskly, she unfolded it, as if she were going about her business, but after one more glance at the beige curtain leading to the front of the store, Teresa slipped the boot box into the bag and walked quickly to the rear exit, the door leading out to the alley and the garbage cans, and there she tucked the bag behind one of the trash bins, inconspicuous, where she would pick it up after work.

It was that easy. When she turned back into the storeroom, it was still empty, Candy nowhere in sight. Teresa was surprised at how calm she was, how she could mask herself in the same way Candy had when Mr. Carson had come searching for her earlier in the morning. She made herself look busy, as if all she'd done was sharpen her pencil and gather more index cards. By the time she ascended the ladder again, Teresa had only the vision of the clock in her head, the small amount of time left before lunch and Dan's soothing presence.

"Teresa," she heard Candy call out. "There's someone here to see you."

She stood on the ladder, waiting for Candy to round the aisle and find her directly, but Candy wasn't budging. Her voice came from the front of the storeroom, edged with jealousy.

"Teresa?"

"Coming," she replied. She shuffled down the ladder and walked toward the beige curtain, where Candy stood waiting.

"You should probably tell him," Candy whispered, "that Mr. Carson would prefer visitors to wait outside."

Teresa pulled aside the curtain, and there he stood with his hat respectfully in his hands, Dan Watson in a pair of dark jeans and a plaid shirt he must have just purchased, the creases still evident where it had been folded. She could not hide the smile on her face, the previous evening's dreaming and the morning's long walk now wiped away, Dan Watson just as handsome as she remembered him from yesterday, his brown hair wet and freshly combed. The hat, she realized, was a measure of respect—he hadn't actually worn it, judging by his hair—and when she recognized the gesture, she found herself catching her breath.

But Mr. Carson looked over to her and held her gaze long enough to bring her back to her senses. He stared at her as if she should have known better, though there were no customers in the store.

"Are you ready for lunch?" Dan asked.

"Yes, but at noon sharp," she answered, almost swallowing her words. "Mr. Carson?" She approached the sales counter, putting her hand on it when Mr. Carson did not look up from his work. "Mr. Carson, this is Dan Watson."

"He's introduced himself," Mr. Carson answered, not looking up. "I knew his father."

"Yes, sir," Dan said, a little uncertainly.

"You can go at noon on the dot," Mr. Carson said, not looking up. He finally raised his head and, without a trace of hesitation, said to Dan, "I don't like my employees to be picked up at the front door, especially in front of customers. There's a door in the alleyway."

"Yes, sir."

"She gets an hour lunch and cannot be late."

"Yes, sir," said Dan. He backed away toward the door, Mr. Carson's fingers back on his ledger, and Teresa watched him exit.

She was about to turn to the storeroom when Mr. Carson spoke.

"Never again," he said.

"Yes, sir," she said, and pulled aside the curtain. Her meekness gripped itself into a flush of anger at Mr. Carson's behavior, the embarrassment at being ordered to be picked up from the back alley when she'd seen Candy leave from the front many times at the end of the day, her sweet boyfriend picking her up.

"Don't be late coming back," Candy said as Teresa gathered her purse. "I can't go to lunch until you return, you know."

"Of course," she replied, and headed for the back door, wanting to turn back to see if Candy was eyeing her, relieved that Dan had not yet driven up the one-way alley, a skinny passage of broken pavement and splintering utility poles, trash cans, and yellowing weeds. Her Carson's Shoes bag sat exactly where she'd put it, pristine, and without a second thought, she took it up by its looped handles.

"What you got there?" Dan asked her when she climbed in.

"I've been saving for something special," she said, one hand still on the loops of the bag. The lie slithered out too easily, and she turned to look at him as if he suspected her. She took a peek at the side mirror, half expecting to catch a glimpse of Candy bursting out the back of the store, her deed discovered.

"We can get a burger," he said, "since you don't have a lot of time."

"That sounds wonderful," she answered. He flicked the

signal to turn left. "But could you take me home first?" she asked. "To leave my package?"

"It'll be safe in the truck."

"I'm sure it will. But I don't want to have to carry it home later. And I don't want to bother you with keeping it for me."

"It's not a bother," he said.

"No, really . . . ," she said, and already she could feel the heat of her own protest, as if he would immediately suspect what she had done, what she was willing to do.

"Sure thing," he said, flicking the signal to turn right instead.

Dan drove along the streets at a comfortable pace, Teresa nervously clutching the bag. *I know you. I know about you.* People went about their business the way they did every day. She looked out at them as the truck eased on by. She couldn't get to the apartment fast enough. It would be one thing to get inside her room with the package from Carson's, but this panic was going to be much harder to shake.

"I hope this isn't going to be a quiet lunch," Dan said. "You're like a mouse."

She clutched the bag handles one more time, took a deep breath, and then eased her hands, letting go. "It's been a long morning," she said.

The truck stopped at an intersection, and into the crosswalk came a woman in a brilliant yellow blouse and fitted gray skirt, elegant and unhurried. She was escorted by a tall man in a crisp white shirt, though he wasn't holding her arm. They crossed in front of the truck, the woman turning to acknowledge Dan's patience, and Teresa saw him give the woman the slightest nod. Teresa watched them go. How easy it was for a woman like that: the lack of complication in her life was almost an air around her. Someday, Teresa thought, the beauty of a marriage like that would come to her as well, like opening a window, and there would never be a feeling of being watched or judged, stared at in envy or suspicion or even desire. If anyone looked at her, it would be from admiration.

Such a grand plan to dream like this. Why wouldn't love come easily? They eased onto her street. The Mexican men on the corner spotted her in the truck, though Cheno was no-where in sight. Something inside her stirred at the thought of him, the inevitable moment when she would have to tell Cheno how things had changed.

The Mexican men stared at her as Dan parked the truck, and she realized they would be the ones to tell Cheno, even if it wasn't the truth the way she would tell it. Dan kept the motor running and she went to the door, package in one hand, key in the other. They followed her with their eyes. They knew her. They knew about her. They knew all about her.

Seven

By the time the Director and the small crew reached Bakersfield at two in the afternoon, even the Actress knew that the day was wasted. A flat tire had delayed them on the drive over from Los Angeles, and the whole reason for coming—a quick day trip for rear-projection road shots and site scouting—had to be rethought. They would have to shoot the scene first thing in the morning and, if time allowed, have the photographer set out on his own with specific instructions about what to look for.

The Director phoned her room. "Would you have an early dinner with me, say about five thirty or so?"

She agreed, and when she met the Director downstairs, she was surprised when the clerk stepped from behind the desk and showed them to a small room off the lobby—a meeting room, she realized, for the oilmen who came through town. A few round tables sat unadorned, but one was covered with a simple tablecloth and place settings, and the clerk led them to the chairs, pulling one out for the Actress.

"You can take away the third setting," said the Director. "My wife decided to rest instead."

"We can have a plate sent upstairs if you'd like."

"Just soup," said the Director. "And salad and bread. Very light. She's not feeling well from the trip."

"Is she all right?" asked the Actress.

"Perfectly fine. More agitated than anything else after sitting in the car all morning."

The clerk poured them each a glass of wine, but the Actress put her hand up before hers was full. "I didn't know the hotel had a kitchen," she said to the clerk.

"We don't, actually," he responded. "A few dishes are coming over from Ruby's Steak House, just down the street."

"I hope you don't mind," said the Director, "but I went ahead and ordered for you. A steak, medium well, and a little salad with dressing on the side in case it's too tart, as some dressings tend to be."

"It sounds lovely," said the Actress, nodding at the clerk.

"Send my wife a bottle of this," said the Director, having sipped the wine.

"Very well," said the clerk. "The food will be here shortly," he said, and exited the room.

The Director unfolded his napkin and sighed, clearly agitated. "What a waste of a day."

"It must be frustrating."

"We won't have a lot of time. Or money. When the full production starts, I'll have little patience for setbacks like this."

"I was explaining to the driver during lunch that our shoot had to take place in the morning because of the quality of the light."

"You had lunch with your driver?"

"Yes," she answered. "At the café just across the street."

"He did nothing untoward, did he?"

"Of course not!" She smiled at his suggestion.

"Of course not," he said. "That's a good man, after all. It's not polite to let a lady eat alone." He seemed to recall the loss of the day's work and shook his head. "If we'd been here on time, we could have had a lovely lunch somewhere with my wife. She would've been in good spirits, too. Good company. She enjoys yours very much."

"Enjoys what, exactly?"

"Your company. She's a smart lady, my wife. Very sharp. She appreciates intelligence in others. She says it radiates from you. Starlight, if you will."

"That's very generous of her."

"Oh, come now," he said. "Take a compliment."

They both turned at the sound of the doorknob being handled almost apologetically, as if the clerk didn't want to interrupt them, and he peered in as if to announce his presence before wheeling in a cart.

"I'm famished," said the Director. The clerk served them the plates, the steaks simple and a bit thin, but steaming hot, the bread warm and covered, in a small basket. The Director sliced into his steak with a guarded delight, not taking a bite until the clerk exited once again, and if he was unhappy with the tenderness of the meat, he didn't let on.

"It's too bad there isn't a window in this room," she said. "A little natural light would've been nice."

"Yes, indeed," he said. "I'm grateful the hotel had such a room available. It would've been most intrusive to go out

unannounced to a restaurant and have a gawking public watching us eat."

"Oh, they'd recognize you, but not me necessarily."

"I don't believe that for one minute. They surely would. Did
no one do a double take in the café when you had lunch?"

She smiled. "Perhaps."

"I would think so. Small towns are filled with people who
notice every little detail. They make the best kind of audience
in some ways, limited as their viewpoints might be."

"I'm a big-city girl now."

"Sophisticated," the Director agreed. He served himself a
little more wine, and even though the Actress had not touched
hers, he moved to pour the rest of her glass. She did not stop
him, not wanting even her small gesture to appear disagreeable
to him in any way.

"Yes, indeed, sophisticated," he said. "You know, it pleases
me quite a bit to hear you talk about light."

"Light?"

"The quality of the sunlight. Explaining to your driver why
we absolutely need to shoot in the morning to keep to the
script."

"I think you may have mentioned that to me at one point.
Something about the angle of the sun in the sky and the
shadows."

"Precisely. Some people are quite discerning when it comes
to natural light. They have an eye for it. They seek continuity.
If a scene takes place in the morning, the eye wants morning
light. The best critics especially. They look for any reason to

dismiss a project outright. That's why I'm so meticulous about setting and being proper about it." He looked at her. "That doesn't make you nervous, does it? Does it make me sound demanding?"

"Not at all," she said. "It's to be applauded, I would say."

"I'm guilty of judging a picture harshly myself. I can't bring myself to forgive even television. One evening, I was watching an episode of *I Love Lucy* with my wife. Very harmless and comical. Do you like her?"

"Oh, very much so."

"She's a genius really, though I have to tell you that, as a director, I wouldn't know what to do with someone who is so gifted physically. It's a whole other element to bring to an already complicated task. In any case, the episode had Lucy and her friend planning to steal John Wayne's footprints from Grauman's Theatre in Hollywood—"

"I remember that episode. She was quite funny!"

The Director laughed. She felt relieved to hear him let loose, a good, wholesome chortle, easygoing, and it made him lose the sharp edge he had, the silent, watchful scrutiny that she had already observed from him in their previous meetings. She ate a little more freely and took some of the wine.

"Very funny indeed. Yet as I was watching, I was appalled that such a marvelous sketch had such terribly shoddy sets. When the two girls get ready to steal the footprints, they hear someone coming, so they hide in a set of bushes tucked to the side. Pure convenience! I know Grauman's. They have no such landscaping. And that got me thinking about the time of day.

They were stealing the chunk of sidewalk in the evening, yet the lighting was incorrect, and there was hardly an effort to disguise the fact. Inexcusable, even if it is television."

"It didn't ruin your pleasure, though, did it? You still found it funny, no?"

"I enjoy a good slapstick, so, yes—my wife and I enjoyed the episode very much. But my point is the respect you must give to the discerning eye, to people who know how to look rather than just see." He eyed the room, studying the walls and the simple decor, not a shabby dining area by any measure. "Serviceable, don't you think? For a city this size?"

"Absolutely." She looked at the walls, painted deep blue, and the white wainscoting ringing the room. She watched in surprise as the Director lifted an edge of the tablecloth and knocked at the table, as if listening.

"That's good solid oak for a modest room."

"They don't skimp around here apparently. It's a lovely meal, isn't it?"

"Suitable," he said, and they ate silently for a moment, enjoying the food. "I'm very glad," he said, "that you made the comment about not having a window in this room. I like your attentiveness."

"A little light would've been nice. I always like to know what time it is."

The Director glanced at his watch. "Say, we have a little bit of daylight left. Would you like to do some scouting with me, out on the west side of town?"

"The west side?"

"The motels. We can compare our findings with the photographer's work from this afternoon."

She agreed, and while they didn't rush the rest of the meal, she begged off another glass of wine, eager to get on with the Director's invitation. When the wardrobe mistress had spoken to her about the brassieres involved in the first scene, she'd told the Actress that she'd been asked to go around Los Angeles and think carefully about the undergarments that a secretary's pay could afford. So here was a chance to be, strangely, just like the set decorators, to engage in the level of scrutiny they'd been asked to apply in their study of young women's apartments in Phoenix. The details might even take the burden away from the difficulty of her performance.

They thanked the clerk at the front desk and stepped out front, where Carter, the driver, was smoking a cigarette. He stamped it out quickly and opened the car door for them, and the Director instructed him to drive out to the highway access road, where the motels were strung along in a neon line. The day was giving itself over to dusk, but the light was strong enough to allow solid views of the passing storefronts, and the Actress watched as the shops of downtown Bakersfield went by. The windows appeared small and meager to her, not like the showcases of Los Angeles, but the shops made the most of their space. In a record store window, she spotted the shiny discs hanging from the ceiling like black stars. An appliance store lined up a whole row of television sets all tuned to the same station, and the sedan drove by just as the owner began turning them off, one by one, for the night. A shoe store racked as many pairs as possible on the floor of its window display, leaving the windows open to scrutiny from the outside: a fat man stood at the front counter, chin in his hand, watching two young women scurry with stacks of thin boxes.

Gradually, the businesses turned over to gas stations and animal feed shops, small lumber stores and farm equipment repair barns, all of the various places that made up, as the Actress recalled from her own youth, the everyday landscape of small-town life. As Carter drove them out toward the access road, she got to thinking about her secretary character making a run for such a town, the desire stirring within her to seek love with a man who ran a hardware store, a business that could turn hardscrabble in a drought year, given a town like this. She pursed her lips at her own imagination, the extension she was granting to the story's parameters. "If setting is so complicated," she said to the Director, "I can imagine why you don't want your players to overthink their roles."

"Actors can interfere to a degree if they overplay. I don't like actors placing too many emotions that aren't there. It's the audience that should feel sad or frightened or angry, don't you agree? I think I've done my job well if the audience responds in that way."

"If I may be so bold, then," she said, "what, really, is there left for me to do, as an actress?"

"Well, your character has done a terrible thing. You've lied and you're a thief, yet I want the audience to have some sympathy for you, to always consider you the heroine. Even when the police are chasing you, I want the audience to be rooting for your escape. How you do that will be up to you. I don't know anything about acting. I just know who's right for the part. Instinct tells me. So do the terms of the contract."

She chuckled. The driver slowed down as he approached a cluster of motels, each of them announcing themselves with large neon signs already turned on against the coming dusk. The Mountainview, which faced north to the flat stretch of the rest of the Valley. The NiteNite and the Anchor Motel, surrounded on all sides by dirt and gravel.

"The Mountainview has a big, handsome sign," said the Actress. Its large blue neon arrow descended straight down, narrowing to a point that curved to the driveway entrance and the motel's name in bold white letters.

"Lovely facade," said the Director. "It looks like what you'd picture if one said the word 'motel,' don't you think? But the name's all wrong."

"I like the sound," said the Actress.

"It's not the sound. It's the name. If I showed that sign on the screen, some fool in the audience is going to wonder where the mountain is."

The Actress turned and pointed out the back window. "There's a mountain there."

"No, no," said the Director. "You had to turn around to see that. It would break the composition to show that angle. You want the approach from the road, the motel sign, and then what happens in the motel. No one cares about the road scenery on the way to the place." The Director leaned forward to get a better look at the other two motels. "Let's go farther along the road."

"What's wrong with these two?"

"The NiteNite is a terrible name for an inn. Doesn't sound very classy, does it? Even for a truck driver. And a place called the Anchor should be near water. Florida, cotton candy colors, and all that."

Not much farther down the access road, a large, assuming rectangular sign came into view: WATSON'S INN, it read, and the Director tapped on the front seat to get Carter to slow down.

"Should I pull in?" Carter asked.

"Why not?" said the Director, even though the driveway was quite close to the front office. The driveway was level with the road, rather than sloped downward as at the other motels, and though the parking lot looked tight, there was plenty of space for larger trucks. Two long buildings sat at V-shaped angles to each other, facing the traffic, a front porch running along the entire length of each facade, the windows of each room with curtains pulled back to let in the light. In the gap between the buildings, a glimpse of two more units facing the other direction, away from the road, quiet.

"This one is perfect," said the Actress with assurance.

The Director stayed silent, but he was clearly taking it in. Carter idled for a moment before the Actress nodded at him slightly to put the car in park and cut the engine. When the motor shuddered quiet, the silence broken only by the occasional passing car, the Actress knew she'd picked the right one.

"I do hope the photographer spotted this one," the Director said. "You've got a good eye."

Over to the side, from a small house with its facade angled toward the motel buildings, a screen door swung open, and a woman stood on the steps looking at them for a moment before starting down to greet them.

"Driver, we should probably get along and not bother this woman," said the Director.

"That's awfully rude," said the Actress when Carter turned on the engine. "We can politely tell her we're leaving. She's making her way down here."

"You have a good eye," said the Director, "but I can see you've never had to deal with people."

"Cut the engine, Carter," said the Actress, rolling down the window. She stopped midway when she got a look at the woman coming toward her. Was it the color of the woman's waitress uniform? Or was it the way the woman looked back at her, a slight hesitation in her step at the recognition, even though the window was rolled down only halfway. She could not, the Actress knew, stay half-hidden, and so she continued turning the handle until the woman could see clearly into the car.

There was a point when the woman knew exactly who the Actress was, and she stopped almost midstride, close enough to the car to speak without having to raise her voice.

"You . . . ," the woman said.

The Director leaned in to the Actress to whisper as low as he could. "You know this woman?"

"Good evening," the Actress said, but her words came out with a nervousness she did not intend, and she could see the woman bend down a little to see who else was in the car. She seemed a bit taken aback when she saw the Director in the backseat.

"You're movie people . . . ," the woman said.

"Yes," said the Actress. "You see, we're in Bakersfield scouting sites for a new film . . ."

"I asked you in the café if you . . . ," said the woman, shaking her head. "You lied to me."

"I apologize for that. I really do," said the Actress. "It's something I must do, just to be in public."

The woman folded her arms. Though she stood a bit away from the car, there was no mistaking that she was small framed, her thin brown hair pulled tight in a bun, her eyes souring at them in distrust, her mouth pursing downward. "Do you know you had all those young girls riled up? I'll look like an old schoolmarm for telling them to hush up about you."

"I really do apologize. I hope you understand."

"What is it you're doing out here?" the woman asked. "On my property."

"Well, we're scouting sites for a motel—for the film—and this looks like a superior location, compared to the others we've seen in the area."

The woman leaned a bit to take a look at the Director, but the Actress could feel him settling back in his seat, as if he didn't want to speak at all. The woman glanced at the driver, her uncertainty and suspicion only deepening.

"Let her know we compensate," the Director whispered.

"We'd pay you a bit," said the Actress. "Just to look at the rooms and the layout. Take a few pictures. We can send someone out tomorrow."

The woman made as if to go back to the house, dropping her arms from her body, shaking her head. She turned back to them. "I don't think so."

"May I ask why?" the Actress called out after her.

"To be honest," said the woman, "I don't like dealing with liars."

"Tell her we'll compensate handsomely," the Director said.

"I do think we could manage a nice compensation," said the Actress. "For all your time."

"You Los Angeles people . . ." The woman shook her head. "You think money solves everything. You're so goddamn money-grubbing. You could've just rented a room and scouted all you want when I wasn't looking."

"Just let her go," said the Director.

"Thank you for your time," the Actress said, and started to roll up the window.

The woman took a few steps back toward the car. "You know, if you hadn't lied about who you were . . ." Her voice rose as in a pitch of anger, firm yet cracked through with a pain so apparent that the Actress wanted to hold the sound in her fingers, a small, angry pulse in her hands.

"We're very sorry to have bothered you, ma'am," said the Actress, rolling up the window with a rush, muffling the woman's words, and she urged Carter to get them going.

The woman reached the car and rapped at the window with a flat palm, but they couldn't hear what she was saying, and Carter pulled away with enough of a rush to kick up some of the gravel, the Actress staring straight ahead in a bit of embarrassment, yet at the same time filled with a need to turn back to see how the woman had been left standing.

"Awfully defensive," said the Director. "Whatever was she talking about?"

"In the café," said the Actress. "She was our waitress, the hostess. Did you see her, Carter?"

"I did, ma'am."

"What was she angry about?" asked the Director.

"She recognized me and I told her she was mistaken," said the Actress, and yet while she saw that such an exchange shouldn't have warranted such a reaction, something else about the woman lingered with her, a strange understanding.

"So unpleasant," said the Director. "In any case, I'm sure the set decorator can put together a typical room from a few photographs. It's an easy layout to copy. Flat, rectangular. Nothing complex."

No, the Actress thought, not complex at all. Carter drove them back into Bakersfield. She put her hand to her forehead and leaned against the door, sighing audibly as if she were tired, and the Director took the hint. The ride back was quiet. She thought about the woman, her fierce response to their presence, to her small white lie. What kind of person was she to react with such defensive hurt? she wondered. The woman was a café hostess, but what was she doing at the motel? Was it a second job? No, not if she was still wearing the uniform. Perhaps she was the wife of the man who owned Watson's Inn, an unhappy marriage, given the way the Actress had noticed the woman casting glances at her and Carter during their meal. The woman had tried to figure out if she could place her as a Hollywood star, to be sure, but she had also paid mind to the way she set down the plates in front of Carter, her eyes darting quickly to his face as if to gauge if he was pleased. A café waitress. A wife. A motel owner. A harried café waitress. A lonely wife. A desperate motel owner. She spun the words in her head, more and more of them, inventing, watching Bakersfield come into view. Who could live in this city? What brought or kept them here?

The Actress thought of what she'd discussed with the Director that evening, about exteriors and brevity and visual cues, and she brought all this to bear on her character, the Phoenix secretary. A Phoenix secretary was not enough. For simplicity's sake, yes. But a Phoenix secretary had an interior, too, a heart filled with dark hope and longing after she'd looked at a photograph and with justifications she'd made while lying awake in the dark. The Actress would not gloss over these things, however much she had to invent them, have hints of it flash across her face. *It's all in the eyes,* the aging silent actress had told her many years ago, and she was discovering that this was truer than she ever thought possible, that the aging actress had been talking about more than just beauty all along.

Part Two

Eight

The months went on and things did not change. October rolled on through November, the December gray finally blocking out the sun. As the year wore on, Arlene took notice some days of how the morning looked through the plate-glass windows. How did Bakersfield ever get through the summer heat, the intolerably white sunlight? The only thing changing was the season, but who paid attention to that? Not the girls chattering along and unfocused while the customers waited for coffee. Not Dan, still seeing the young Mexican girl from the shoe store, sometimes even daring to come into the café with her, her little shoulders sporting a new winter jacket. What could Arlene do? Did she want things to change? The farmers noted the change, though you couldn't tell from Vernon, who still came in during the late morning, or Cal, who joined him at the counter not fifteen minutes later. They bantered with her, and the exchanges were mechanical yet soothing to Arlene, like listening to a clock. No, not much was changing except the weather, the seasons, Arlene ending her café shifts at five with the streets nearly gone dark. Her Ford was a serviceable '52, but the engine doubted itself more and more as the chill of evening settled deep all around her. She made the nervous drive home with a certainty that her headlights would fail, but they, too, held on. It was a change she wouldn't have wanted—the need for a new car when winter was making money scarce all around the city.

More and more, once she got back to the motel, she would find the parking lot empty and Dan nowhere to be seen. He'd taken up with that girl enough to sometimes close the front office too early in the evening, the motel mostly empty. Who knew how many customers had driven away when no one answered the knock at the front office? Tonight, the parking lot was empty for a weekend, and she knew even before she pulled up close to the front office that Dan had already left.

Every once in a while, back at the café, Cal would read the latest news about the new highway, and she would keep up her nonchalance, acting as if she wasn't already alarmed at the current downturn in business. What was it? The lack of paint? The two new motels nearby that had come up that summer? Was her rate in line with the rest of the city? She thought about how much worse it would get if the highway diverted the traffic away, as Cal kept insisting it would.

Things change, she thought to herself, though this was a slow, creeping change, like water seeping underneath a door.

This evening was going to be like every other evening. Dan had purchased a TV for her from Stewart's Appliances, a hefty color set to appease her for his absence, but it was a complete waste in her mind, since half the programming was in black and white. These days, she'd come home from the café so exhausted that, with Dan not around to cook for, she had started buying those new frozen dinners. Turkey with gravy, corn, cranberry sauce, and rice that didn't taste half-bad. She sat in front of the set and found a teleplay about to start, a story set in New York City about a young couple struggling for money and living in a cramped apartment, the husband a drunk who staggered around. His voice blared out of the speakers so loudly that Arlene had been tempted to get up and turn down the sound. Something was strange about the story, these city people struggling like small-town folk, when everything she'd seen about the big city dazzled with easy luxury. Arlene watched with mild interest, turning every once in a while to the parking lot, which remained empty of customers, until she realized that the characters were never going to leave their shoddy apartment, were never going to step out into the glamour she'd seen in magazine spreads. She turned the set off, wrapped a sweater over her shoulders, and walked out to sit on the porch.

Those were the days, she thought, when she could feel change coming. Sitting on the porch as a little girl, her mother trying to retell a story, but all along they had been waiting for her brother. She rubbed her arms against the chill, but it wasn't just the cold—it was the knowing, the thought of her young self anticipating her mother's anxiety, wanting to live with it somehow. How had she known such a thing, at her age, going out to the porch at one in the morning because she knew that, come dawn, her brother would be standing at the edge of the dirt road that passed in front of their farmhouse, the Sierra Nevada bright gold in the east, and her mother running to him, crying and smoothing his hair just like she had done to Arlene, and no one in the family saying anything about where he had been?

What would her brother have made of how big Bakersfield had become? He had gone off to Los Angeles after his release from prison, but he had never returned. Just like her husband, Frederick. Her brother had left so long ago that hardly anyone remembered that she had a sibling. She thought of this, how she hid the fact under her tongue, how she rarely told anyone that her own blood had once been in prison. She remembered how everyone from the nearby farms had gathered in the early afternoon to welcome her brother home, his long bus trip from up past Sacramento to Bakersfield. They had led him to the backyard, and the men sat squat-style in a circle, drinking beer, her brother the beginning and the end of the loop, the one who balanced on his haunches the longest without having to get up to stretch. "Prison will harden you to stand anything," he had bragged, the men laughing, but his voice carried over to her and settled inside like the smoke from his cigarettes, one after the other. He lit one up as a signal to the rest of the men that he didn't feel like talking, that he'd rather listen to the stories of their years, all that time he'd been locked away.

How much time, Arlene thought as she stared out at the empty parking lot, had he actually been gone?

Those men had spent the entire afternoon like that, the sun coming down and the men still talking, the cigarettes glowing in the dusk. There had been a lot of ground to cover. There had been a lot of ways to say how unfair her brother had had it.

Come along, her mother had said, her hand on Arlene's head. *It's getting late.* Night had come. The ashes in the pit had died down, the food long ago eaten. All the men stayed, dark shadows with dark orange glows.

Arlene had heard them as she lay on the floor in the living room, her eyes once again looking out past the open front door of their old farmhouse, past the porch, and fixing on the dark road outside. The men's faint talking filled her with a vague comfort, knowing that the dark was not so lonely.

When she had opened her eyes, it was dawn. The front yard was quiet. Her mother was not yet awake. Arlene rose and walked to the kitchen, the open back door. A light dew on the grass, beer bottles strewn everywhere, and the men long gone home. She had never even heard them leave.

Down the hallway, the door to her brother's room was wide open. Arlene stood in the quiet of the house, looking down the hallway, a chill that she found soothing in the morning air, how it had seeped inside, the doors open for the cross breeze. She stood long enough to listen to the house settle, a creak in the wood somewhere in the roof. She stood and looked down the hallway at the open door to her brother's bedroom, wondering if he was actually in there or if he'd gone off with the men for more drinking. The answer was right there, just a quiet tiptoe down the hall, the door already open. But instead, Arlene kept standing there, taking in the unfamiliar and delicious chill to the morning air. She was understanding that it did not matter if her brother was in that room right then. Her mother loved him. All that mattered was that he had returned and that life was going to change in their house.

Things change. Everything's gotta change, Arlene thought, rubbing her arms, and she stepped back into the house.

But how some things stayed. That feeling, standing in the hallway. She could remember it even now.

It was early yet and Arlene was tempted to turn the TV set back on. She was in no mood, though, for another unhappy teleplay, and instead she prepared for bed, turning off the lights in the house one by one and taking one last look out at the parking lot. With some guilt and some defeat, she turned off the motel's road sign, a little angry that Dan wasn't around to man the office in the evening hours like he had agreed. But no one was coming. She lay in bed and tried to get her mind to stop racing, to stop thinking of the motel's demise, and in her frustration she put her hand out to the empty side of the bed.

Sleep came in a strange wave of images: Cal at the counter turning the pages of the newspaper; Vernon drinking from his coffee cup; the young waitresses wiggling their bottoms for the farmers. Sleep brought the Actress, too, enough to wake Arlene a bit to near alertness, wondering what had become of her, Cal never having seen anything in the newspaper headlines announcing a film shoot. She floated back into sleep, her mind flitting from image to image and refusing the clean slate of dreams, a sound thumping and thumping until Arlene opened her eyes, groggy, and realized the sound was real. She sat up, alert, and listened carefully as the faint thump came again, from Dan's room, and she recoiled for a moment at the possibility that Dan would dare bring that girl into the house when the motel rooms sat empty and secretive.

She listened for voices but heard nothing except Dan's footsteps and drawers being opened and shut. Her nightstand clock glowed a surprising five minutes past eleven.

"Dan?" she called from her open room. A light shone from underneath the door to his room. "Danny?"

The noise in his room stopped for a moment, and Arlene stood at the threshold of her bedroom, waiting to hear an answer, wondering why Dan was taking so long to respond when he had clearly heard her voice.

"Dan?"

He opened the door and stuck his head out, the same brown hair as Frederick's, the same hard line of a nose. The same long jut of clavicle and the coarse ring of hair around the nipple. She caught a glimpse of his white underwear. She remembered Frederick's coarse laughter when she had told him about her brother, about having no idea where her brother had gone during his first night home.

"What's going on?"

"Sorry, Mama," he said nervously, his body half-hidden behind the door. "Go on back to sleep."

"If you have a girl in there . . ." Arlene teetered between stepping forward and stepping back. She braced herself for the embarrassment of confronting a naked girl sitting on the edge of Dan's bed. She steeled herself as she had when Frederick shushed her, Dan's little-boy footsteps in the hallway, tiny and fearful.

Through the sliver of open door, her view partially blocked by Dan's body, she saw the edge of the bed. It was bare.

"What's going on?" she asked again.

"Mama . . . ," he protested, but the absence of the girl allowed her to approach the door insistently. It was her house. Then she saw the suitcase.

"Where the hell do you think you're going, Dan?" She put her hand on his door and he pushed back. She was surprised at her strength, but knowing she couldn't hold her ground, she slid her hand on the jamb, fingers in full view, daring Dan to close the door and bruise her.

"Mama!" he yelled. "Leave me alone!"

"You better not be running off!" she yelled back. "The two of you are too young to be doing that!"

She pushed harder against the door—hard enough to surprise him, a peek of his face coming through the sliver of doorframe—and she gasped at the similarity of his face to Frederick's. But then she spotted the cuts.

"What's that on your cheek?" she demanded. "Dan, answer me!" She put her hand on the jamb, fingers laid out as fragile as eggs. She felt him stop pushing on the door, a silent truce.

"Mama," Dan said quietly, "give me a minute to put on some clothes. Okay?" His voice was jittery, now that she heard him speak a complete sentence. "Okay?"

"All right," she agreed, but she kept her fingers on the jamb. She heard the rough slip of Dan getting into a pair of dungarees, the slide of a drawer as he searched for a shirt. Then he slowly opened the door.

Dan's suitcase sat open on the bed, a story she didn't yet know. Next to it was the black bank deposit bag from their front office. He stood with his hand on the doorknob.

"What's that on your cheek?" she asked, but now she didn't want to know the answer. A black eye or a crust of blood under the nostril or a swollen lip would have made it easy to imagine too many beers at the Bluebird, the inability of men to keep their mouths shut against bravado. Dan's cheek was something more dreadful in its simplicity: four little half-moons, caked in purple. A small hand doing that to his face.

"Something happened, Mama . . ."

"Oh, dear God . . . ," she said, and took her eyes away from the scratches on his cheek and saw the mess, the spilled contents of his bureau and, on top of it, his white shirt with dark stains, the deep, ugly sheen. She couldn't help but touch it, her fingers electric against the damp, and she flinched. "Oh, dear God . . ."

He was a blur of motion, hurrying over to the suitcase, gathering the black bank bag and shoving it inside, snapping the thing shut. She followed him out helplessly, incredulously, as he made his way to the kitchen, pulling the cabinets open and yanking down bread, boxed crackers, a jar of peanut butter, a tin of canned meat. In a flash, he spied the keys to her sedan hanging by a hook near the door and grabbed them before she could stop him.

"Dan . . . what on earth happened?"

"Listen, Mama," he said, stuffing the keys into his pocket. He became calm once again, the tone in his voice suggesting he was not going to repeat himself. "You listen to me, now. I'm not telling you where I'm going. And I'm not going to tell you what I did." His voice quivered and broke. "You know what I did."

She thought of her brother, after all that time in a prison upstate, and the way he took a cigarette in his mouth and blew out the smoke.

"What did you do, Dan?"

"Listen to me! The police are going to come around here soon enough. So I'm not telling you anything. You don't know anything, so they can't call you a liar." He patted his pocket, as if to assure himself the keys were there, then reached under the sink for a paper bag and gathered the food.

"Dan, you can't do this . . ."

"Mama . . . ," he said sternly. "I took the cash from the office and I'm sorry about that. But you get rid of that truck. Okay? Take it up into the mountains and burn it or push it into the river. Just get rid of it."

"I won't do any such thing," she said, with a firm voice, a glimmer of defiance, the same tone she had used when speaking to Frederick those years ago in this very kitchen, when he threatened to leave her if she didn't stop pestering him about his late hours. Frederick had looked at her with a stare as thin and deadly as a razor.

"You do what you want," Dan said. He gathered the food and the suitcase and butted his way to the front door, unstoppable, and she wanted to reach out to him, remembering how her mother had reached out to her brother to embrace him when he came back.

To her surprise, Dan put his things down and hugged her. He held her hard and she allowed him to. She closed her eyes against the half-moons on his cheek, their ugly certainties, and willed everything to stop, to stay as it was.

"I'm sorry, Mama," he said. "I am." He gathered the suitcase and the paper bag of food and bounded out to the parking lot. She ran out to the porch, almost following him down in her bare feet. She watched his dark form fumble with the keys, heard the click of the door as he unlocked the sedan. The night was still, no cars on the highway, no sound at all, the entire city

asleep, and her car roared to life, startling her. The inevitability startled her, the coming change. The motor gunned and the
lights, weak willed and scant, dimmed as Dan put the car into
reverse and wheeled right out of the parking lot. Just like that.
Just like Frederick, whom she had not witnessed leaving, only
finding an envelope on the kitchen table announcing his depar-
ture. The envelope held the deeds to the motel and the house
and a bit of cash, but otherwise no indication about where
he had gone. But the dark silhouette in the sedan tonight was
not Frederick—it was Dan, making a hurried right turn onto
the highway, heading south, the red taillights disappearing, the
rumble of the engine receding, and Arlene on the front porch
alone and looking at the dark.

Dan's black Ford pickup stared at her, parked lengthwise,
its one visible headlight a wary eye. It sat there like a still but
breathing animal. The truck spooked her, a dark hulk in the
empty space of their parking lot, and Arlene had to step away
from the door, a foolish fear of the truck somehow turning on
and idling there. It reminded her of falling asleep in front of
the television set and waking up to static that unnerved her,
filled her with a shaky dread as she rose from the armchair and
moved toward the set, deeper toward the source of her irratio-
nal fear, just to turn the thing off.

Sooner or later an officer would indeed come and park his
patrol car in front of her house, stepping out with questions.
The truck sat out there with the inevitable answers. She wondered what was in it, why Dan wanted her to dispose of it. She
pictured herself driving it east of Bakersfield, on any of the
roads that headed out on big, easy asphalt, then meandered

into swerving, near-single-lane passages that hardly anybody traveled. Not this time of year, with fog and sometimes even snow in those hills if a cold front came in hard. Those were summer roads, roads for fishing spots along the creek, bass and trout making their way down the Sierra, picked off all along the way until only the lowly catfish survived. The hills blazed with dry grass but by winter went green again and even muddy, the tree trunks rich with moss. Hardly anybody went up there, just the locals who knew the roads. No guardrails to stop a vehicle from plummeting down into the ravines that grew deeper and deeper as the hills gradually turned into mountain.

She could see herself doing it.

She could see herself driving the truck up there, the hairpin turns of those roads. Far up there. Ten miles, maybe, of that kind of driving, then pulling over and turning off the engine. And then what? A box of matches and a jug of gasoline? Would the truck explode? She could see it, the truck blooming in flame, consumed. Would anybody hear it, the echo of the blast, somebody looking east and seeing an odd orange glow over there in the mountains way before dawn? The orange tip of her brother's cigarette glowed when he puffed, its blaze a signal that he didn't want to talk anymore, just listen. Would the truck burn itself out, or would the flames leap over to the grass, the damp winter containing it? What then, with a ten-mile walk back to town? How long would that take, especially in this cold, her hands huddled around her elbows, her feet against the asphalt in thin shoes? The little girl in her childhood picture book walked all that way. But how impossible! Five miles, then? Three? Just far enough away from the eastern edge of

Bakersfield, at the beginning of the hill slopes, far enough away
to slip the truck into neutral and steer it over the side of a ravine, out of sight of the road.

For what? It was nothing she had done. She had no lies to
conceal. She knew where Dan was headed. Only south. And
that was logical. Over to Los Angeles to hide in that enormous
city. Over to San Diego. To Tijuana and everything she'd heard
about its teeming, ugly life.

She didn't even know what he'd done, really.

The truck stared back at her, and she stood on the porch for a
long moment, the way she had stood in the early morning hallway of her house when her brother had returned. She had been
waiting for answers back then. Right in front of her, the truck
held them. She went back into the house to wrap herself tight
in a housecoat, and she slipped on a pair of Keds. She walked
down the porch stairs, the truck beckoning like a faithful star.
Her eyes fixed on the cab, its interior too dark for her to see inside. What was she expecting, the body of the dead girl? Arlene
chided herself for being so afraid, never having been so, after
all these years near the highway, so far away from town, having grown up in the countryside. Darkness was just not being
able to see. Nothing came out of it. She had stared at darkness
throughout her childhood summers as she'd gone to sleep, the
strange noises outside nothing but small animals foraging for
food. Yet here she was, approaching the truck with so much
timidity that she felt foolish.

She opened the truck door, the dome light dim, and ran
her eyes over the interior. What had she expected? A torn and
bloodied bench seat? Red handprints on the steering wheel?

Nothing seemed unusual, nothing that demanded the truck be destroyed as Dan had adamantly suggested. Maybe, Arlene thought, it was simply that the police would be searching for the vehicle, that someone had spotted it making a getaway from whatever horrible scene still waited to be discovered. She needed the truck now, Dan having taken her car.

But then she spotted something. The dome light was too dim for her to see clearly, so Arlene leaned in. Along the curve of the steering wheel, along the ridges made for the fingers to grip, she could see a vague discoloration, a darkness. Her stomach gripped in panic, the fear coming again, and she stepped back as if shocked by an electric wire.

"Stupid, stupid, stupid," Arlene muttered, anger overtaking her fear, wishing Dan had driven away in the truck instead of her sedan. Now what was she to do? She looked at the steering wheel more closely, her eyes following the curve and spotting the rest of the marks, streaky, as if he'd already tried to wipe them away. Fearless now, Arlene put her finger on the wheel, expecting to feel something slick or dried, but nothing was discernible, just the cold, smooth surface chilled by the December night, and the keys still in the ignition.

"Stupid, stupid . . . ," she muttered again. She eased onto the bench seat, the door still open so the weak dome light could give a measure of guidance. She spit on the steering wheel and, with the inside hem of her housecoat, began to wipe away. She spit into her hand and ran it along another spot, working the hem along the steering wheel as if she were fastidiously wiping down the café counters, the task of cleaning always something she could put muscle into. Arlene turned the hem of the housecoat and inspected it, the fabric now tinted with a deep color. She wriggled out of it, impervious to the chill of the vinyl seat, and spit a few more times on the steering wheel, on the dashboard, swiping her housecoat along the surface with a confused vigor. Why was she doing this? What, exactly, was she trying to hide? It wasn't her story to manipulate, not her words that she needed to consider carefully when the police came looking. She stopped wiping for a moment, considering. She looked at the inside hem of her coat, the newly dark smears on the cloth, but then turned the hem down, the coat back to how it looked every day, and decided then and there that Dan was on his own.

You know where he went that night, right? Frederick had asked her when she told him years later about her brother, about wondering where he'd gone that first night after getting home. They'd been lying in bed, very young, when being in bed was still thrilling and exhausting, and Arlene had her hand on Frederick's chest. She could feel in her palm the deep, guttural cackle he let out when he asked the question, a pulse so disconcerting she had to take her hand away.

He was out getting pussy, Frederick had said, laughing, both of them in the dark, and she was grateful now, sitting in the truck, that she had not seen the look on his face when he had said that. *If your brother was in prison for three years, believe me, that was the first thing he went out to get.* Her brother, who had shown up at her wedding at City Hall all cleaned up, a poorly fitting suit picked out from the secondhand shop on Union Avenue, but cleaned up nonetheless. Sober, clean shaven, his hair combed, freshly cut in the kitchen the day before. Hardworking, too,

stacking fruit crates on the farms up north by Exeter and Por-
terville, picking strawberries and almonds, driving trucks. All
the love shown to him by their mother, only to find that he'd
left all the hard work and gone off to Los Angeles, never to
return.

That was one unlucky woman, Frederick had said. *Whoever
she was.*

Dan, she thought, her own son, was ripped through with
that same ugliness, the same disregard, as her own brother,
whatever was contained in the pulse rooted in her palm, holding her hand against Frederick's chest as if she could keep his
ugliness at bay.

The parking lot sat silent, greeting her revelation. The
night sat silent. Nothing moved. Not even a cold breeze to
disturb the trees. Nothing from the highway. Not the truck
still settling with metallic pings. Not even her own breathing.
The windows of the house beckoned to her, but not warmly,
not the yellow picture windows of her childhood storybook.
They stared back at her with a cold, white gleam, and inside,
Arlene knew, were years of empty rooms.

From the road came the sound of a distant motor. A truck:
she could tell by its downshifting gears, the way the engine
sounded as it approached and slowed. Arlene looked in the
rearview mirror, but then came the distinct sound of brakes
that needed a tending to, and the soft arc of headlights sweep-
ing left as if preparing to make a turn into the parking lot.
Hadn't she turned off the lights to the motel's road sign? She
quickly closed the door to the truck to shut off the dome light,
one eye on the rearview mirror.

Sure enough, a diesel truck turned a slow roll into the parking lot. Its headlights swept over the cab and glistened on the chrome and glass, refracting, and Arlene edged herself against the door. She held her breath as if doing so would send the truck away, but it eased over to the edge of the parking lot, near one of the motel wings. The truck sat chugging for a moment, and Arlene listened, not able to hear anything over the noise of the truck's idling engine, and unable to see much in the rearview mirror. Maybe the driver was studying the darkened motel office or looking at the still-lit windows of the house, judging whether it was worth it to disturb anyone at this time of night.

The engine idled interminably and then suddenly stopped. The parking lot was plunged back into silence—she could even make out the diesel truck's engine ticking away as it cooled. It was too late, she realized, to step out of the truck, even if the driver might make nothing of it. But later, when the police came and maybe questioned him, it would seem suspicious, her getting out of a truck, housecoat over a nightgown. She craned her neck to get a better look in the rearview mirror but could see nothing in the darkness, and then the door to the diesel truck opened.

The sounds carried. The weight of his body as he jumped down to the ground. A gob of spit as he hacked to clear his throat. His boots stepping across the gravel. Another door opening and then the rough whisper of his voice saying something in the dark—were there two of them? She listened for an exchange, but it was only the driver's voice. He was talking to himself as she heard him step onto the wooden porch in front of the motel office, then rap on the door. Arlene heard him knock again before he let out a whistle and an admonishment that she couldn't make out: that was when she made out the soft footfalls alarmingly near the truck and realized the driver had let out a dog. She could spot its dark form in the side-view mirror, lifting its leg to whiz on the truck's rear tire. She stayed absolutely still, even as the dog sniffed its way along the side of the truck, as if it sensed her inside. The dog paused for a moment, its attention held stone-tight at her window, and it let out a short, anticipatory growl.

"Buddy!" she heard the truck driver call out in a hoarse whisper, then a quick, sharp whistle of a command. The dog obeyed, but she could see the dark form of its head still fixed on her as it trotted back toward its owner. One more time, the driver let out a short whistle of admonishment, as if the dog had stopped to rethink its retreat, and then the parking lot went silent again.

In the mirror, for the briefest moment, she saw a tip of light, as if a firefly had flown into view. She wanted to rub her eyes to see if she'd imagined it, but it came again and this time she caught its orange color, the tip of light she remembered from her childhood, watching her brother. He was smoking. She shifted a bit and turned to take a sidelong glance out the back window. The tip of his cigarette bloomed a few more times. He was too far away for her to see his silhouette in the darkness, to know whether he was facing the road or staring up at the cold light of the house, deciding once and for all whether he would make the effort to knock up there.

Two glows later, the orange tip darted to the side and went out as the driver flicked the butt to the gravel. She heard him whistle softly again, but the dog seemed near its owner, the whistle calm and reassuring. The driver's boots shifted across the gravel, heading back to the diesel truck, but then he paused yet again, this time urinating—a heavy, long stream hitting the ground before the boots resumed walking. Arlene could see the light in the truck's cab turn on again as the driver opened the door, his voice saying something to encourage the dog to get inside, and then he lifted himself back into the cab.

Arlene sighed, relieved, and ducked back a little, anticipating that the headlights of the truck would sweep over her again. She crouched down, waiting, but as the moments slipped by, the truck didn't move. She kept anticipating the engine turning over and the truck getting back on the highway to search for another motel. But nothing. "Sweet Jesus," she muttered when she realized the driver was bedding down for the night, the silence growing deeper and deeper. She braved another sidelong glance through the rear window, still fearful that the driver might suddenly turn on the engine, the headlights catching her like a fox in the road. The truck remained still. Nothing passed on the highway.

The tension in her body hardened further in the December cold. Arlene could feel it in her fingers. She wouldn't last much longer, dressed as she was in her nightgown. She draped the housecoat over herself and sat up a little straighter, craning for a better look at the truck. In the other direction, the front door of her house seemed impossibly far away. She racked her brain trying to recall if she'd locked the kitchen door on her way to bed earlier that evening—maybe sneaking around to the side of the house wouldn't rouse the driver or the dog.

But now everything she did, Arlene knew, would carry a sound, just like the driver's boots, the dog's prowl of her premises, the driver relieving himself on the ground. The dome light of her truck would turn on, but maybe the driver wouldn't see it, now that he was bedded down for the night. She would have to slip out of the truck quietly and click its door shut, then scurry up the steps to the house.

He could be exhausted and already asleep. He could've drunk a beer or two on the road just before he made the turn-off, the alcohol making him drowsy. But how many nights had she herself been awakened by movement in the parking lot, one of the drivers who'd checked in going right back out to the Bakersfield bars?

Her feet numbed at the toes. She could not wait much longer.

Arlene took a deep breath. She grabbed the door handle, absolute ice to the touch, and held it for a long moment. Maybe it would be best to put the coat on first. She slipped it back on, arranging herself, and was surprised at how much noise she made by doing so. She shot a last look back at the diesel truck, but nothing, so she took the door handle once again and this time pulled.

The dome light blazed like an accusation, and she scrambled as quietly as she could out of the cab. The truck door groaned. Her feet thudded onto the gravel. Alarmed by the noise she was making, she shut the door as softly as she could, the dome light extinguishing, but she couldn't hook the latch. She pushed the door a little, finally hearing it click shut, but she could see, even in the dark, how the door wasn't flush with

the frame. From the diesel truck came the faint but percep-
tible growl of the driver's dog, alert to her movement. Arlene
crouched down, listening for the growl again. She imagined
the dog sitting up in the seat, paws resting on the door, studying her malevolently through the window of the cab. Her body
ached from crouching, the slumped posture, the cold. Just that
pathway to the house, just those steps, just the screen door,
just the twist of the knob. The dog remained silent, as did the
road, so Arlene bolted, trying her best to half run, half tiptoe to the house, the cold gleam of the windows taunting her
with their proximity, but by the time she hit the steps, she was
so overcome by the fear of being caught, by the anticipation
of the driver calling out *Hey!* into the night, that she disre-
garded the creak of the screen door and how it always slapped
against the frame, and rushed in, shutting the door behind her
hard enough for the window to shudder.

Yet even after she made it inside, she kept looking out, with
the same foolish impulse that forced her to run back into the
house on some mornings to check the electric coffeepot, its
unplugged cord coiled safely away. The trucker had remained
asleep, the dog not barking, and she turned out the living room
light, one window going dark, signifying motion to anyone
who might be looking. But no one was looking. She knew this
now. It was well past midnight and anyone still awake would
be only half so, nodded off in front of the buzz and static of a
television set, the local stations not able to fill insomnia's empty
hours. There was no need to be nervous, but she remained so
as she walked into the kitchen, filling a teakettle with water and
setting it to boil so she could ward off the chill of having been

outside, wondering if her silhouette appeared in the windows, a ghostly form to an onlooker from the road. The ugly feeling was unshakable, that sense of being watched. Arlene reached over and turned out the kitchen light, one more light extinguished in the house, leaving her alone with only the blue flame of the stove, startlingly bright. So bright, she was surprised how easily she could manage a teacup from the cabinet, a spoon from the drawer. At the first sign of a coming whistle from the kettle, Arlene removed it from the stove, carefully pouring hot water by the glow of the blue flame, something to keep her eye on as she sat in the kitchen.

What's a mother to do? Arlene thought. She saw her mother in the Bakersfield courthouse, her dedicated mornings of dressing up in her best outfit to sit through proceedings she could not possibly have understood completely, then coming home in the afternoon to air out the dress and make it ready for the next day. *What's a good mother to do?* Willful and stubborn, sitting in silence while she heard exactly what her own son had been accused of. *What's a good mother?* Arlene considered the chasm she had to cross to be like her mother, to be confronted with the irrefutable, yet still acknowledge her own flesh and blood. A son no matter what. *Here is a knife. Here is a gun. Here is a bloody set of clothes. Here are your son's hands.* Deep down, she knew she could never be like her mother, long dead now. Upstairs, she remembered, was Dan's bloody shirt on the dresser, but now she did not feel the sense of panic. There would be more to dig out of by trying to hide the shirt than by allowing its discovery. She would show the police officers, lead them right to it, her arms crossed over the flaps of her housecoat, and they would never think to inspect her garment and trace it back to an earlier moment of desperation.

Arlene sat at the table, warming her numb fingers against the teacup. There were hard days coming. Tomorrow, would she go to work? Would she be able to simply carry on with the business of the day, serving coffee, swiping change off the tables and dipping the coins into the pocket of her apron, making it clear through her silence that she would not be entertaining anyone's nosy questions? How fast would the talk start swirling? With the patrol officers coming into the café at 6 a.m. on the dot for scrambled eggs and hash browns? Wouldn't her face grow more severe by the hour? Wouldn't her hair, pulled back in a bun, look even more like a gesture of resignation to her coming old age? *Let your hair down,* one of the young waitresses had told her, about six months after Frederick had left her, when it was clear to everyone that the male regulars had gotten wind of her situation. She had felt ashamed about it: feeling abandoned on the one hand, desired on the other. Not good enough for her own husband, yet not damaged at all in the eyes of the lonelier bachelor farmers.

But this was different. How much time would pass before people began to ask her questions directly? How thick would the silence be when she walked over to a table of customers and everyone politely gave their orders? Would it be better or worse if Dan were caught, arrested, and dragged back to Bakersfield? How would it look if he disappeared, Arlene still walking around free? The young waitresses would cross paths with one another in the back kitchen. The whole town would be talking about her. *What kind of mother raises a son like that?*

Sitting in the dark of her kitchen, Arlene wasn't sure if the clarity was real, but she understood her mother now. With her hands on the teacup, she felt for the warmth, its measure, its certainty, the way she had felt the laugh rumble from Frederick's chest, a discovery. She searched her own mind now in the same way, her own heart. What it took to sit in a courtroom when the entire world was against your son. What it took to sit there and know the silent judgment being cast upon you, the way you had to raise your head and walk in and out of the courtroom with conviction. Nothing you could do would bring back the victim everyone was grieving over. Nothing could be done in terms of real justice. Mercy wasn't anywhere in the law. Neither was forgiveness. Or clemency. If it was, someone would have called out and said there were two mothers in the courtroom—why should they both suffer?

Could Arlene do that at least? Walk in and out of the café and face the day with her chin held high? *Mrs. Watson. That woman. Her son.* Long years awaited, whether or not she rose from the kitchen table, went back to bed, or remained sitting until dawn. Ahead were long years of being Mrs. Watson, with no one remembering Frederick, no one remembering she had a first name, even though it was on the red badge she pinned to her uniform every day. A waitress, but no one's ex-wife. No one's daughter, her family long gone. But everyone remembering she was the mother of that young man who had done that terrible thing.

She resolved to stay at the kitchen table until dawn. She

resolved to stay until the police officer came with his inevitable questions. She resolved to point to the room at the back of the house and tell him what was in there. She resolved to tell him about what Dan had wanted her to do with the truck, how she had refused to do so because she was a mother. Arlene looked outside at the dark shape of the diesel truck and felt for the man inside. She had forced him to remain in the cold, huddled uncomfortably with his dog to pass the night, all because she hadn't had the wherewithal to act like a woman first and not a mother, a person who cared about someone else's well-being, not just her son's.

Arlene thought about walking back out there and rapping on the door of the truck, showing the driver to one of the rooms and telling him with great apology that the fee would be waived. She decided against it, only because she was going to be facing life very soon—questions, suspicions, accusations—and these would be the last quiet hours she was going to have.

She thought back to that morning years before, when she had stood in the hallway of their old farmhouse, her brother maybe or maybe not in that back bedroom, and she had listened for some kind of noise to tell her that he was in there. Instead, her own mother rose and disturbed the quiet of the house. *Arlene, honey,* her mother had said. *What are you doing up so early, my love?* And then her mother began making an enormous breakfast in the kitchen.

The hours passed in the dark, Arlene transfixed by herself, by the silent truck in the parking lot, by the huge well of her coming life. The tea went cold. The blue flame burned. When the sky started to change over in the east, she finally rose from the table. She turned on the light. She took out eggs and sausages from the refrigerator, pancake mix from the cabinet. She set coffee to boil. She worked with resolve, remembering how her brother had walked into the kitchen to the smell of their mother's cooking, his hair matted, and he made a playful grab for her and brought her to his lap as a cup of coffee was presented to him. The pans sizzled hot on the stove. *Thank you, love,* Frederick used to tell her, after their big Sunday dinners. Arlene made hearty portions and set everything on a breakfast tray—the coffee in a carafe, the eggs and sausages and toast and pancakes covered with a larger, upside-down plate to keep everything warm as she made her way outside and over to the truck.

The sky readied itself for day in the east. Arlene cleared the steps carefully, making her way to the diesel truck. The December morning clipped her with a sharp chill, her breath in the air. The dog sensed her even before she had taken a few steps, but she kept her resolve. She would move forward. There was only forward.

From the road came the familiar sound of tires, of a car slowing down. As she looked to the road, the police car rolled into view, and she stopped. The dog barked madly and she heard the driver call out, "Buddy!" in a tired voice, then again when the dog raised its paws to the window. The police car slowed down and she could see in the coming clarity that there were two officers inside. They parked the car and she felt her hands go numb. "Buddy!" the driver yelled, and she could hear him rising up in the cab. She wanted to keep going, but the distance was too great, too long, the simple path into the storybook forest too dark, too dark. She felt her hands give up and drop the tray as the officers opened the doors to the patrol car, the food spilling all over the gravel, the plates shattering, the coffee carafe tumbling. Arlene looked at the truck driver's breakfast and then at the two officers approaching and she collapsed to her knees, weeping. She wept hard. She held her face in her hands and the morning was cold and she wanted to go back inside to the safety of her little house with the warm yellow windows.

"Mrs. Watson?" said one of the officers, approaching her. He came in to the café every day, just past the lunch hour, and ordered a grilled cheese, home fries, and a cola. "Mrs. Watson?" he called one more time, his boots on the gravel. He came closer, closer. Then he put his hands on her shoulders and bent down to her. "Arlene?"

Nine

When she entered that room, she thought the difficult moment would be the instant she loosened the robe and let it fall from her shoulders, all eyes on her, and already the need to start acting, to move with a nonchalance about her own body, taking off the robe without it appearing sensual. But when you remove a robe, you remove a robe. There's no hiding nakedness. The moment she took off the robe, she could feel all the eyes in the room averted, and no one witnessing how she handed the robe like a coat to the wardrobe mistress. The eyes averted, but sooner or later they looked at her. She wasn't naked: she wore bikini briefs, and her breasts were mostly covered with a flesh-colored moleskin fitted and glued painstakingly by the costume designer, intended to make her look naked with the proper camera angle, no worry about straps being inadvertently caught on film, or even the pinch of flesh caused by fabric bunching up with the tiniest wrong move. She wasn't naked, but all eyes settled on her because she was the one being filmed, with a proximity of cameras and lighting that she had underestimated.

Their brief scouting trip, back in October, had failed to bring them even the road shots showing the Actress driving her car: they had to shoot those later on a soundstage and add the voice-overs in the editing. Production began after the October trip, straight weeks of tight, rushed work all through the fall. Some of the sequences that involved no actors—like long shots of the Phoenix skyline, or a rear projection of a police car driving along a stretch of desert highway—were completed by an unsupervised second unit, the Director specifying exactly what needed to show up on film. But not this scene: the desire for order was keener, the Director sitting the Actress down and showing her how the sequence was going to be staged and filmed, a barrage of particular shots, each of them choreographed with a precision the Actress found almost daunting in its exactitude. The Director mapped out each shot on board after board, and she could see for herself how he was planning to get around the problem of her nakedness: the trust that the camera would shoot only the particular part of the body he was asking for and nothing else. Her torso, her thighs, her shoulders, the curve of her bare back.

The Actress had studied the sequence carefully. The Director clarified once again the number of camera setups, the lighting changes, even the position of the crew. Already it occurred to her that it would take an enormous amount of time between setups: a glitch in the opening, once her hair was already wet, would require the hairdresser's blow-dryer at the very least. She flipped through the storyboards with a measured, silent alarm, moving past the issue of having to disrobe in front of the crew: she was going to have to be in that state continuously, always reaching for cover whenever the camera stopped rolling.

Last week, there'd been difficulties with the initial set design, a plumbing flaw with the drain and a lack of warm water, clearly frustrating the Director, and it was then that she understood just how attuned he was planning to be to the specificity of his mind's eye, and she thought—of all things—of a painter setting a bowl of fruit on a sunlit windowsill, sketching quickly to catch the shadow of pear against orange, the shallow depth of the bowl, before the sun interrupted the composition.

How fleeting it would all be. She removed her robe and waited for the first of the difficult shots involving water: unwrapping the bar of soap and turning on the showerhead. *There she is, finally admitting to her wrongdoing in her own mind, and she's rinsing all of the bad thoughts away.* This was what she was meant to convey, but the Actress stared at the unwrapped bar of soap sitting on the edge of the tub, doubting if she could ascribe that much meaning to such a banal act. It seemed ludicrous to her now, standing in her moleskin covering and bikini bottom, to be *acting,* almost impossible, given the number of eyes on her. *More and more,* the Director had told her, mentioning Europe and its realism, the shedding of the American style of artifice, and the ever-closer tilt to the vulgarity of everyday life. Goose pimples broke out on her arms when she thought of the water, praying it would come out warm.

The action started and she stepped into the tub with complete faith, the way she would enter an elevator in a tall building and trust the cables to bring her safely down the heights. The camera was positioned just below where the showerhead would be. She pulled back the curtain and bent down to pick up the soap from the ledge, unwrapping it carefully, trying not to be distracted by the microphone near her hands, off camera, capturing the sound of the paper. All eyes were on the task at hand, but still she felt their intrusion, the many hours she would be standing like this in front of them. She turned on the water, a small, almost involuntary grimace as it poured out, a little chilly but not especially cold, and she let it run on her face for as long as she could before the Director called cut, her hands immediately reaching out for a towel, the wardrobe mistress ready with a dry robe in her hand.

All that for a mere couple of seconds of film at best. She sat to wait as the back breakaway wall of the shower stall was removed from its sturdy hinges by the grips. The Actress asked for a towel to dry her hair, but the wardrobe mistress shook her head, the next shot appearing imminent. The camera was repositioned where the back wall had once been, as if looking out to the bathroom door, and when it became clear that the shot setup was going to take some time, the wardrobe mistress finally produced a towel and let out a sigh, the look on her face that of a noticeable need for a cigarette.

The Actress waited, listening to the proceedings and trying to stay alert to help the Director move quickly if he called her to her spot. She saw what they were busy arranging: the camera would face the bathroom door, so it was a matter of light and shadow, not just the blinding surface of a shower wall. The set decorators were on hand with a batch of shower curtains of varying opacity. The curtain was pulled to and fro as the lights waxed and dimmed, the Director shaking his head at what he could and could not see. He called out to her. "I just need to see you in this spot here," he said, pointing, and she rose from her seat, her back hurting already from not even a half morning of doing nothing but waiting. She stood in her spot as directed, her warm robe pulled around, the men arguing over the finer shadings of her light.

At ten, another woman came in and sat quietly in a chair. She, too, wore a robe, but already the Actress knew she had no clothing on underneath—no bathing suit, no moleskin coverings, no bikini. The other woman sat without saying a word, her time being paid for, though it seemed today her services might not be required. Even though she had a robe on, anyone could see she was endowed with a magnificent pair of breasts, hips curved for a Las Vegas floor show, yet she sat in the chair reading a Marguerite Duras novel in French without once glancing up to meet the eyes of the crew, who stole quick glances and grinned at each other.

Not fifteen minutes later, another woman appeared, this one tall and thin, accompanied by more people from wardrobe, a scattering of props on hand while the Director guided the talk about the lighting. The Actress observed them as they positioned the tall actress at the frame of the bathroom door, silhouetting her, discussing the width of her shoulders, the shape of the wig, the appearance of the knife in her hand. For the rest of the morning, the Actress and the Las Vegas starlet sat in their identical chairs, the nuances of the lighting details becoming so particular and technical that they hardly made sense anymore. For the rest of the morning, it was the tall, thin woman who received the direction, who was guided in how to raise the knife menacingly, who was urged to slow down her entrance through the door, even though she was nothing but a shadow.

Finally, when they were ready to shoot again, the Director called for the Actress, and it occurred to her that even the pivotal scene of turning to face her surprising demise was not yet in the cards. It was merely the entrance of the silhouette. "Can we run the water a little bit, just to warm it up?" she asked, and one of the crew answered politely that it was hardly going to get much warmer. Still, they ran the water some, the Director asking her to keep her right arm close to her body as she rinsed, to conceal the shape of her breast from the camera as best she could.

By this time her hair had dried, and the Actress wondered to herself about just how wet her hair had been in the previous shot. She stood with her face under the tepid water for as long as she could before raising her arms, involuntarily, to run her fingers through her hair.

"Cut right there," the Director said. And though everyone could hear him, the Actress felt he whispered what he said next. "I could see the shape of your breast. Keep your right arm down and use the left if you must, but keep the right one down, elbow in."

"Hair?" asked the stylist. "Do you need it dry again?"

"No, just go as is. As if you've been under the nozzle for several moments," he said to the Actress, and the camera rolled again.

This time, the Actress monitored her right arm, the feeling like a constriction. Suddenly the bathroom set seemed oppressively contained, the physicality of the scene becoming like a series of dance steps to be practiced, rehearsed, and replicated with supreme precision. She rinsed her hair, her body contained, but her face registering what it was supposed to.

"Cut. Stop there. Your entrance," he said, before the Actress realized he was speaking to the tall, thin woman. "Open the door, but pause before you enter. Don't rush through."

The water was still running and the Actress stood as far away from the stream as she could. It was getting cold.

"Again," the Director said, motioning them all to start. She stood back in the shower stream, her eyes closed serenely against the water, realizing she wasn't playing the part at the moment, but no matter. She just wanted to hear the sound of the curtain being pulled, but the seconds dragged on. Even before the Director called out for a cut, she knew something had gone wrong.

Something about the lighting was displeasing the Director, and the wardrobe mistress motioned to the Actress to get out of the shower. The water was turned off, the set becoming quiet as the Director conferred with the men around him, until finally he said, a little dejectedly, "Early lunch. One hour."

Half a day and hardly anything burned onto film just yet. Over a sandwich and a cup of coffee, the Actress studied the script again, turning to the pages that described the shower scene, but then she pushed the whole thing aside. For all its audacity, this was a technical exercise, and all she had in her head about this woman's vulnerability, her moment of surprise, and her terror was now revealing itself to be almost irrelevant. When the scream came, it needn't be done with an eye to its believability, but to its function, how she looked when she did

it, if her face was in focus, how she carried her scream over the
sound of the water falling in the echo of the shower. On the one
hand, yes, it was a moment that she knew was different from
other movie deaths. It was real carnage, not an actor going
down in an elegant ballet, clutching his stomach, his face grimaced in perfect pain. In her teenage days back in the Valley,
sneaking into movies midway through a screening, she'd seen
gangsters fall majestically in a rain of bullets, women screaming bug-eyed at a movie monster and raising their hands like
museum statues. But for this scene, something else was at
work, and even the Director's explanations and his revelations
on the storyboards hadn't been enough for her to realize what
he was doing until she had come into the middle of the action.
It was now a measure of camera angles, how water appeared on
the screen, the height of the shot, the overheads, the sound—
her body as a prop—and she finished her coffee and sandwich
and reported back to the set a little early, readying herself to be
used as needed.

   All afternoon, they worked with slow precision. The Las
Vegas girl stood in the shower completely nude, and a different shower curtain, a little more opaque, was hung up to conceal her nipples. Lens condensation corrupted a couple of the
shots when the shower ran too long, and they had to start over.
The back wall of the shower jammed in place and the grips finally muscled it out, their dirty fingerprints wiped away from
the edges to maintain the illusion of a bathroom so pristine it
gleamed. The warm water ran out and they had to wait awhile
to let the tanks reheat. The Las Vegas girl took to sitting topless
so much that even the crew stopped noticing.

The next day, it was the same thing. A new girl, equally curvy and coached to be more demure when off camera, came in as a replacement. More camera setups, failed takes, moleskin applications, arms over breasts with the back almost to the camera but not quite. Sometimes it was the new girl in the tub, doing exactly as she was told while a camera shot from overhead, keeping her head down as much as she could so there was never a possibility of noticing she was a stand-in. She dried off and quickly robed, paper cup of coffee in hand, watching the proceedings. The screaming was easily done, only a couple of takes because the editing would take care of the rest, and all the thinking the Actress had done about the moment of this young woman's death was really for naught. What was more important was how the woman walked into the bathroom, what she was doing right before, the casual way she went about making a grand decision in her life, her effort to change course, and how the certainty of that decision was going to be silently clear to the audience: this was a changed woman, and she was doing the right thing. She was good enough to be forgiven.

It took seven days to shoot the scene, almost as long as it had taken to shoot the preceding drama, and with the holidays so near at hand, the pressure to finish fell heavy on the set. Who knew it was going to be so demanding? But it wasn't the time involved—it was the physicality and trusting that the Director could see what he needed to see. It was the appearance of nakedness without being naked, hard as it was to tilt her body away from the camera when, right out of the corner of her eye, she could always see a voluptuous pair of Las Vegas breasts at the ready.

But in the end, she was stunned at the effect. Sitting in their screening room, never having seen any of the daily rushes, never having seen the rough cut, but now watching the finished film itself—with music!—the Actress hardly recalled that she was witnessing herself. At every sequence, she could remember the Director's hand guiding her through the moment. Her elevated sensuality in the hotel room with her handsome costar. Her face registering the feeling of being pursued and the fear of being caught as she made her getaway. The shadings in her expression as she reveled in her own conniving and cunning while her character listened to interior voices. Even the angle of her head as she listened over a motel dinner of sandwiches and milk, a woman listening to a story, but matching it to her own, comparing it, her disrupted life not ruined at all, but a shiny thing in her hands once again, renewed.

She had become that woman entirely.

The Actress knew it even as she watched her character sit at a motel room desk, her moment of reckoning coming. In a little notebook, she scribbled out the simplest of subtractions: seven hundred from forty thousand. Something she could have done in her head. But she did it because her character was alone and silent, not even a voice in her head, and the audience in the dark needed to be looking over her shoulder as she began making amends.

She tore up the note, about to throw it in the trash, but then turned to look to the bathroom, as if remembering it as the one place where everything vile gets washed or flushed away, the camera gliding along with her as she moved to that space.

She was framed in the doorway of the bathroom, bending down to the toilet.

The camera showed the toilet, pristine and white, but unsettling somehow, a toilet never having been on the screen before, and she soiled it with the torn-up pieces of her crime and then flushed.

She bent down to lower the lid, stepping over to close the door firmly, looking up as if to make sure it was closed, then took off her robe, her back exposed to the camera.

Off came her slippers one by one, the robe on the toilet haphazard, her bare legs stepping into the clean tub, and the curtain pulled back with a quick rush of metal rings.

The Las Vegas girl bent down—they used her shots after all—her nipples hardly registering through the thick shower curtain, but from up above, the Actress knew, the crew had looked down in hunger.

Now the Actress, facing the side wall of the shower—the shot from the first day of filming—her hands up in anticipation of the water, her hands up as if in ecstatic prayer.

The showerhead looked down at her like a giant eye.

The water warmer now, her face in relief at finally cleansing, nearly two days, remember, without a shower, a Phoenix secretary spending a night in her car out in the desert foothills east of Los Angeles.

Her arms to block her breasts, the soap beginning to lather. She was beginning to understand why the Director asked her to turn slowly to the left. Patiently. Even taking a shower requires technique. You don't just stand. You turn to wet every part of the body. *Turn,* he had said. Slowly. *Clean.* She tilted her head back like a ballerina.

It came closer to her, the camera. Her head back like a dancer's. That's what she'd been thinking, but what it did was show her neck, offering it up to what was coming. *Keep turning. Slower.*

The showerhead, as if observing quietly, the way the crew had, respectful even though they had wanted an eyeful.

Then the camera, as if it had magically sat on the back wall of the shower, more water coming from another nozzle a little above, like a second curtain of water. *Keep turning. Other direction now. Slower.*

And there it was. When she had stood in the shower, anticipating. When the body double kept stumbling in too loudly; when they oiled the hinges on the door to a smooth silence. A silhouette coming with a horrific certainty that the Actress herself hadn't been able to see from her position. A terrible silhouette darkening the frame, the Actress deliberately moving out of the camera's eye as it closed in on the curtain. The menace of the silhouette terrifying her even now as she watched herself on the screen.

Up there, she turned around from her slow, deliberate dance.

Up there, the camera cut in close as she screamed.

Up there, the camera cut in even closer to just her open mouth.

A silhouette in women's clothes, and a big butcher knife. Any knife will do in real life—a pocket blade in a street-corner mugging, a sharpened screwdriver in a jail cell. But this was the movies and it had to be a butcher knife.

The knife came at her like a tiger's paw reaching through a cage, not able to strike, but the illusion was the same.

The silhouette brought the knife up.

What was (or wasn't) a Las Vegas breast.

From overhead, it was heartbreakingly easy to see how she had nowhere to go, trapped as she was on all sides.

More screaming. *Keep your face in the water. It will force you to shut your eyes.*

Her hands over her breasts: an effort to conceal herself, the Actress knew, but now it read like a gesture of futile defense.

Her own open mouth. She hardly remembered screaming that loudly. Or for that long. But the sound editing made it interminable.

Her hands over her breasts: but by this time, no one in the audience would be thinking of breasts.

The silhouette bringing up the knife yet again.

Put up your hands now. All five fingers.

The silhouette, even closer. The head of a monstrous woman.

Her head moving side to side, as if to say no.

The only thing the knife ever cut through was the water.

Her hands up, but nothing to hold on to.

The knife coming through the veil of water even more forcefully, tearing through it as if it were flesh.

No, no.

When you bring down the knife, he had told the double, *hold it like so. I want to see the glisten of your fingers holding it. I want to see the fingers.*

The Las Vegas girl's naked torso. A dancer turning to her left to meet the knife at just the tip. Not a breast curve or a pubic hair in sight. Not even blood on the knife.

No, no.

The arm still coming down. The knife in silhouette because by this point it would be dripping in blood. Not even all that water could wash it clean so quickly.

The Las Vegas girl kept turning, her breasts visible to everybody on the set, but on the screen, just the curve.

No, no. The futility of no.

She'd stood in ketchup, movie paint, and all manner of liquids, the special-effects guys watching how it pooled around her feet, mixed with the water, and here it was. Chocolate syrup—but in black and white, it was a terrible river.

Start dancing. To the right. Slowly.

She sees herself face the back of the shower wall and clenches in her seat as the knife comes down, despite the pantomime.

Her feet turning, the river churning now in deep, horrible color.

I want to see the fingers. Show me the fingers. She showed them, and there they were, out of focus.

The silhouette exited the bathroom forcefully. An angry, venal exit.

Her hand again, extended like a starfish. And now she saw the power of repetition.

Keep your hand there and turn slowly. She did so with a look of resignation, her body slumping into the tub.

Reach out. Extend all your fingers. Hands did everything here: tore up, cleansed, revealed, resisted, murdered. Now it was a single hand, reaching, with nothing for it to hold but the shower curtain. The Las Vegas girl, her breasts barely in focus.

From overhead, like before, it was easy to see she'd had nowhere to go. Yet it had happened, the way God looks down at everything and lets it happen.

The hooks on the shower curtain popped off in release, twirling around the shower rod, one by one, like dancers releasing their movements in sequence.

She slumped near the toilet, the hardest part of all, the rim of the tub lodged in her ribs.

The showerhead looked down at everything.

The blood streamed down, second by second, the tub being rinsed clean. It spiraled into the drain, disappearing.

And then her own eyes, in a close, tight focus and a slow, painful pullback, trying not to blink. But it had been worth it, her face frozen in the stupor of cruel death, the close-up of her eye. A spiral, a circling. The slow dance in the tub repeating. Such brutality meant erasure, a cold, unblinking eye, a woman lying in a pool of her blood, which was draining away, vanishing. The bathroom in near silence, save the flow of the water, as the camera glided over to a newspaper concealing the stolen money.

The Actress watched the rest of the film in disbelief, terrified at the shock, but strangely satisfied at her last, unblinking appearance, her face registering—for the first time she could remember in a film—that a death meant something. An absence. There was something unsettlingly gorgeous about the slow spiral of her eye, the movement gradually coming to a finish, the way a dance ends.

She wasn't in the rest of the picture, and yet she was.

At the close of the film, she stood up proudly as the people in the screening room—the other stars, some of the crew, some of the studio people—congratulated one another on a job well done. She knew she had nailed it. A death scene, what every actress wanted. Even if it wasn't a hospital, a slow and wasting disease.

This had a dark beauty to it. The character worked because of everything that had come before, the suggestion she'd granted to her in the quiet, strange flashes of feeling across her face. The Actress shook more hands, proud, grateful. Might this ever come again, the chance to make a woman out of nothing but words on the page? The woman had to live before she could die. It was as simple as that. Even if it was the vulgarity of real life—the needs and the mistakes, but also the desire to correct them, the effort toward a forgiveness of herself. A woman like that. All those lonely hours. All the things people do to try to escape.

Part Three

Ten

W hen had she picked up the habit of faithfully reading the
Los Angeles Times every day? Not the Californian, the
local newspaper she glanced at while at the kitchen table or
in the motel office or swiping down the café counters, but the
print from over the Grapevine, the pulse of the large city but a
couple of hours away. At the café, Arlene had always been left
to clean up the discarded copies of Modern Screen and Look
that the girls left behind, and for a while she took these home
with her on the sly, the magazines tucked into a paper bag in
case anyone saw her slipping out the door with the very gossip
she chastised the girls for believing. And people were watching her, after all. Back then, in the initial days after the news
spread about the dead girl and Dan's involvement with her,
Arlene thought she would never live down the heavy stares
in the dining area of the café. Arlene volunteered for kitchen
cleanup and washed dishes and bused tables, kept herself
moving, all to avoid those eyes. In the kitchen's break area, she
swept up the girls' cigarette butts and candy wrappers and, at
first, stacked the magazines neatly in a corner. As the months
went on, Arlene found her voice again—the stern, somewhat

prickly voice she was capable of—and when the girls found the magazines gone one day, none of them dared ask what might have happened to them.

The pleasure she took in the magazines, she knew, was nothing but escape, yet maybe for the first time, sitting in the armchair of her living room, flipping through the pages of a *Photoplay*, Arlene knew what the girls of the café might be dreaming about, why they were moved by picture after picture of movie stars posed with one leg pivoted forward, jewels haloed with gleam. All of this taking place just over the Grapevine, another way to live altogether, the dust giving way to red carpet and camera flash and expensive champagne. Sometimes, in the pictures of the much younger starlets, she could almost see vague semblances of the café girls, similarities so sharp that Arlene felt she, too, could imagine their regret over living in Bakersfield.

The local paper, carrying word of her own real world, appeared on her porch every day and remained there, curled up with its rubber band, yellowing after a few days of going uncollected. She knew what the paper said. She had a life much more regrettable than the café girls did. She stuck to the magazines: perfectly useless information, but a needed distraction from the local news, the chatter that went on in the café as she ran plates under hot water. What ran in the newspaper was not rumor anymore as the days went on. Truth was confirmed. It was true that the girl had no family in town and that there was no one to claim her. It was true that Dan had fled and no trace of him had been found. It was true that he had beaten the girl to death in the dark stairwell leading to her apartment above the bowling alley. It was true that a Mexican was deported, though everyone knew he had had no involvement in the death whatsoever.

Other things were true as well: Arlene did not know where Dan had gone, though sometimes she felt as if the town didn't believe her. It was true that the girl was the daughter of a woman who used to work in the café years ago, around the time of the earthquake in 1952, but so much time had passed that people couldn't even remember where that woman had gone.

Arlene knew what was in the local paper better than anyone else did, yet her eyes never left the glossy movie magazines, seeing the same pictures, the same stars, over and over, as she leafed through the pages day after day. Would the news about Dan ever go away? Would the feeling of being stared at in the café's serving area ever lessen, the silent accusation? At home, she would pause and put down the movie magazine, close her eyes. But there was no wishing away what she had to face.

"You're faster than the young girls," the new shift manager had said, almost two months after Arlene had taken to volunteering to do anything that would keep her in the kitchen. "I need you back out front." The shift manager was in his late twenties, but respectful of her. Without prompting, he called her Arlene and not Mrs. Watson. Arlene liked this about him, as if he wanted to let her know that he didn't think of her as anyone's mother.

His voice was fraught with his own need for help, but she could still detect the kindness underneath it. "Those girls," he said, "are too slow to handle anything all by themselves."

At first, put back full-time at the front of the café, Arlene felt on display, charging briskly by customers without saying a word, aware of the large plate-glass windows and the people walking by, maybe staring inside at the woman who worked there. Her fingers trembled sometimes from nerves, jittery in anticipation of the arrival of the police, coming to break the news of how they'd captured Dan. The deputy who used to come in daily for a grilled cheese, home fries, and a cola stopped doing so, as if to spare her the discomfort. It was like that for a while—all jitters, forks slipping out of her fingers, one time being spooked so badly by the glimpse through the plate glass of a Bakersfield officer coming along the sidewalk that Arlene dropped a whole tray full of dirty dishes.

But things change. She had always told herself that on particularly difficult days. Things change. People would forget. People would find other things to whisper about. Who whispered now about her husband having left her? Who even remembered? Most of the bachelor farmers who used to give her the eye and the sweet talk stopped doing so, their heads dropped over their plates as soon as breakfast came. That had to do, she knew, with her getting older, not with her being divorced, not with what had happened to Dan.

Spring came, the light sharper in the window, Arlene walking across the street, where she could drop a few coins into the aluminum stand for a copy of the *Times*. During the postlunch afternoon lull, she would read with increasing interest about the world outside Bakersfield: catastrophic earthquakes in Chile, missiles firing into the skies above the vast oceans, the threatening pulse of the Russians, border skirmishes in Africa becoming near blooms of war. The rubble of the world clouded

out her own. She let her eyes rest on sports scores, the colum-
nists eagerly awaiting the baseball season. She read of Kennedy
and Johnson, a photograph of Stevenson's bald head reminding
her once again that, indeed, the years had passed, even though
her mind insisted on marking time only from the murder in
December. It couldn't be so, she told herself, and opened the
folds of the newspaper to bring the world in. Sometimes the
arts beat covered the passage of a traveling photography ex-
position, and Arlene began to read of ancient pottery and me-
dieval paintings with a mixture of awe and regret that such
things existed in the world and she had no way of seeing them.
European dance troupes pranced across Los Angeles stages,
and after more than a few afternoons of making herself read
the reviews, another kind of regret began to manifest itself,
too: that she could understand, at least a little bit, the measure
of argument and feeling that went into such reviews, and that
the most joyous of them sparked in her a thirst to see a thing
with her own eyes. When that feeling bubbled within her, she'd
smooth the newspaper flat on the café counter and look up, the
harsh light of Bakersfield coming through the plate windows.
Spring had changed to summer.

The heat appeared to make everyone forget about what had
happened in December. In June, the bowling alley put up a new
neon sign, so big that it obscured the window of the apartment
above, the place where that girl used to live. Sometimes, Arlene
would drive by, urged on by a need to see a light on in the window, some sign that the landlord had rented the apartment out
again. She was within the safety of her own vehicle, and yet
she looked up warily and with a bit of shame, only to see the

window always dark and empty of a curtain or a shade, as sure
a sign as any that, months later, the apartment remained still
and bare.

Was she the only one who knew this? Was everyone forgetting? As much as she wanted the town to forget, she found
herself helpless at the thought of such obliteration, the world
overwhelming everything it could contain. The wide pages
of the newspaper brought story after story, and even in the
middle of summer, when she politely declined the telephone so-
licitation to resubscribe to the town newspaper she never read,
Arlene was certain that even the story of the girl was fading in
the minds of everyone in town, tumbling past rumor and into
the darker jaws of complete erasure.

People left her alone. By July, most of the farmers regained
a distinct comfort around her, and those who remained for a
leisurely cup of coffee in the afternoon borrowed sections of
the *Times* and spoke with her about Cuba and Nixon and the
Chicago Cubs and the resurgent Germans. More and more of
the men took the front section and the editorials and the sports
columns, but she tucked the arts pages under the counter, her
own private and more mature version of the daydreaming the
girls still did over their movie magazines. The cinema postings
sometimes boasted full-page advertisements for films soon
to premiere in Los Angeles, the ink so profuse that it rubbed
black on her thumbs, but Arlene liked the way she thrilled to
the promise of a coming film, along with the attendant glamour of its premiere. She knew it would be weeks before the Jack
Lemmon picture arrived in Bakersfield, and that the Ital-
ian films, with their curiously abstract but beguiling posters,

would never show up at the Fox, but she scanned the advertisements daily whenever a weekend approached, as if the films
themselves held something extraordinary in the promise of
their arrival.

One day, that Actress's face appeared in an advertisement.
The lettering of the film title cracked itself over the page,
spread jagged like a plate dropped and shattered on the café
floor. The Actress looked over her shoulder, mouth agape in
a silent scream. Arlene studied it for a moment before raising
her head from the counter and looking over at the booth where
she remembered that Actress sitting. It was empty now, but she
could see her clear as anything, her kind face somehow able
to communicate her need to be left alone. And yet there she
was on the page, the advertisement's crooked terror a stark dis-
missal of what Arlene thought she knew about that Actress,
passing through town.

The next day, the same advertisement appeared in a larger
size, the silhouette of a foreboding house added to the background. Arlene hadn't bothered, the previous day, to pay attention to the cramped credits running along the bottom, but
today, because of the larger size, she could read the names, and
when she spotted the Director, she saw, as if it were just yesterday, that man's face peeking out at her from the backseat of a
nice sedan.

If this was the film they had been shooting, she had no idea,
then, what they could have wanted at her motel. Houses like
the one in the silhouette didn't look at all like those in Bakersfield, where the roofs sat low and the buildings wide and long,
the better to open doors for a cross breeze. She looked at the

silhouette of the house, how easy it was to read its implied menace, then thought of the single, bare window above the bowling alley. She had to stop herself from thinking that Bakersfield wasn't a place that spelled anything out in cracked letters.

After work, she drove by the Fox to see if the film would be playing, but nothing was showing except a negligible comedy and a western, films she knew had shown briefly in Los Angeles with hardly much interest. Things came slowly to Bakersfield. At the Fox, she got out of her car to see the posters behind the coming-attractions queue, but nothing showed of the Actress's movie, and she walked back to her car and pulled into the quiet streets where nothing much ever seemed to happen. Her quiet town. She lived here. She had never left.

The film would come soon enough, she knew, and she resolved to see it, but when the deep heat of August arrived, the film with the menacing house had yet to appear. This was the loop she'd drive: first the silent apartment above the bowling alley, hoping for a light in the window, then to the Fox, hoping for the film. Nothing changed.

Then one afternoon she spotted an earnest but cheap bouquet of flowers at the foot of the green door to the apartment: she pressed the accelerator firmly without looking again, not wanting to catch even the silhouette of the person who may have been trying to remember that girl, and she knew, too, even before she arrived at the Fox, that the Actress's face would be looking out at the Bakersfield street from the movie poster, her silent scream over her shoulder. Sure enough, when Arlene rounded the corner, the film had arrived.

A small line of people had queued up to see it, and she joined them without hesitation. Every other woman in line was not only young but with a man—a date, a husband—but Arlene was alone, still in her waitress uniform, and if anyone from town recognized her, no one made a motion. The patrons were a younger set than most at the café, not at all like the farmers or the farmers' wives, not at all like people who might have whispered behind her back about how Dan Watson had now been missing for almost nine months. They were here to see a film, young people who didn't bother with busybodies who whispered with the Western Union clerk to see if Dan Watson might be getting secret money transfers in Mexico. They lined up at the refreshments counter for popcorn and candy, Arlene slipping into the screening room and taking her seat as quickly as she could.

It had been a long time since she'd been to a picture house. It had been years—since Frederick—and when the screen lit up, Arlene startled at the bright white, the scope of what she was about to see, and she remembered that bubble of anticipation. This time, though, the anticipation had been replaced by a sense of confirmation, that her deep suspicion of the Actress and the Director would reveal that they had been up to something—exactly what, she didn't know—but as the credits cracked across the screen and the film score jittered the audience, she felt even more certain in her desire to maintain the anger she had felt against them that day. The film—she felt it in her bones—was going to confirm it.

But when the screen read "Phoenix" rather than "Bakersfield," and the camera's prying eye brought her inside a room that looked nothing like her highway motel, Arlene let go of the righteous grip she'd held on her purse, but then tightened it again: she felt fooled by the Actress—brazen in her underclothes in the very first scene of the film! All along, Arlene had thought she would see her motel or even a replica of it. For all her hopes of seeing her place on the screen as a confirmation that she existed in the world, the story was set in Arizona, a woman in a bra and a man bare chested in a hotel chair.

Arlene almost stood up, indignant, but thought of all the young women in the audience, all the young men, and their silence behind her meant they didn't mind at all what the Actress was doing on the screen. Arlene wouldn't fool any of them, walking up the aisle with a nonchalance that suggested she was merely going to get a box of chocolates, so she sat and watched the Actress. Arlene quieted her mind enough to listen rather than just watch, and she learned that the Actress was playing a secretary deeply in love with the bare-chested man. She listened as they declared themselves to each other, thinking of Frederick, remembering the man who had sat across from the Actress that day, wondering if this might even be the same actor now. She saw immediately the Actress's dilemma, the wish to be with a man she loved—what an old story—but there was no way in which they could be happy.

What did a search for happiness have to do with jagged letters and the dark silhouette of a house and the Actress screaming silently over her shoulder?

The Actress in her bra. The tittering of the young people in the audience, all behind her. Later in the story, an arrogant rich man flaunting money, drunk from an afternoon lunch. Arlene couldn't picture the farmers at the café doing such a thing, though a small dot within her knew better. All kinds of people did things just like what she was seeing on the screen. The Actress eyed the rich man's money, and Arlene knew she would steal it, her ugly confirmation coming in the form of the Actress plotting an escape from Phoenix, clad once again in her bra. Arlene thought of the newspaper's film reviews, the dance shows it touted, the traveling photography exhibits, the whole world of art set before her on the pages without ever hinting it could contain such crude ideas within it. Near nudity and adulterous affairs and now stealing. She could hear the young people in the audience laughing in nervous identification with the Actress as she made her way away from Phoenix, evading a policeman staring back at everyone in the theater with enormous reflective sunglasses, the jittery film score reviving yet again as a rainstorm drove the Actress into a dangerous situation. Yet Arlene still couldn't find the nerve to get up.

When the Actress finally pulled over, putting a stop to the music, putting a stop to the rain, Arlene saw what was, in essence, her own life, right there on the screen. The long porch of her own motel. It wasn't her motel, exactly, but an image of it, as if she'd closed her eyes to remember where she lived, out by the old highway, and there, up on the blank white canvas, the screen had called back at her with the best it could do to mock what she knew by heart.

The porch light. The doors. The way the porch sat a little high off the ground. The front office as the anchor to the rest of the building wing. It was her place. Hers! It was what the Director and the Actress had come to see.

And yet it wasn't. Arlene wanted to turn around and say

something aloud to the young people watching, if they had
even bothered to notice that the Actress had been moving from
Phoenix and past Los Angeles to nowhere but Bakersfield.
None of them could possibly know that motel on the screen,
its front office filled with strange stuffed birds. She had no such
thing! Her son was not a thin, cowardly type holding a tray of
sandwiches and milk. That story he was telling about a mother
who was losing her mind was absolutely false.

All the young people sat quiet, listening to the thin coward
on the screen, and Arlene listened, too, her hands on her purse,
but finally she rose to her feet when the coward put his eye to
a peephole in the wall, and they all saw, yet again, the Actress
in her underclothes. Yet again—and in a bathroom! She'd had
enough of such filth. Arlene rose to her feet and walked with
purpose up the aisle, the silhouettes in the dark leaning to see
around her. She could hear the pull of a shower curtain and
she grimaced at the audacity of people like that Actress, people
like that Director, people who reveled in adultery, in bras and
cleavage and hairy chests, in theft, in deceit, in madness, in nakedness, in peepholes and lurid spaces. Arlene pushed her way
through the velvet-padded door of the screening room and out
to the plush carpet of the lobby, no one out there except the
clerk at the concession stand.

"You can't come back in, ma'am," the clerk protested when he
noticed that Arlene was heading for the exit, but she paid him
no mind. She clutched her purse even harder when she heard
a burst of screaming from the audience, but she moved on, not
turning around. She was missing the answer, surely, to the jagged titles on the movie poster, and the screaming continued

faintly, a hint of laughter even as the door to the Fox closed behind her. Who would want to know such things? She stood in
the early evening of Bakersfield, the street lined up and down
with the other patrons' cars ready to take them home.

What a change—to go from the dread of being talked about
as the mother of Dan Watson to stupidly wondering if the
young people in town would think of her as a woman offended
by a film, stomping out in indignation.

She went to work the next day and faced her usual stoic customers, looking for some sign that one of their sons or daughters might have mentioned seeing her at the picture house, but
no one said a word. She set late-breakfast plates in front of Vernon and Cal as she always had. None of the young waitresses
asked if she'd seen any films lately. No one said a thing.

All the days could do, she realized, was roll along. For all
her shame in admitting that the spectacle on the screen had
embarrassed her, no one actually cared. She was nothing but a
shadow in the dark.

Over at the girl's apartment, no other cheap bouquets ever
showed up, and she began to wonder if there might even be another story attached to the one she had seen. Maybe it hadn't
even been left in memory, but was the remnant of a date gone
wrong, some young people at the bowling alley, perhaps.

August passed. The fall came, with the light softening in the
window. December rolled past, and with it the first anniversary of that young girl's death, but no one looked at Arlene in
silent knowing. Not the other waitresses, not Vernon, not Cal,
not that young deputy who would come in for a grilled cheese,
home fries, and a cola.

People were going to forget that girl, Arlene realized. Just as they were beginning to forget her—Arlene Watson.

The days kept going. She spread the news of the world on the café counter and watched the stories swallow up her hands, ink all over her fingertips. The light stung in the windows again, announcing spring, anticipating summer.

"Has anyone come to see you about your motel, Mrs. Watson?" Cal asked.

It was July. It was 1961. She looked up at Cal.

"You've been asking me that question for years, Cal."

"The planning is over," he said, pointing to the newspaper. "They're building."

She had known they were. She didn't let on that she had stood on the edge of the motel parking lot, shading her eyes west. Past the fiery line of sunset, she could see nothing but empty space there, a horizon pulled taut. She didn't know what she had expected to see—cranes, maybe, or the elevated ramps and thick pillars of highways like she had seen on television.

"Why would they come see me?"

"Are they anywhere close to your property? Could they buy you out?"

There hadn't been much letup in her motel bookings. Sometimes weekends were slow, but that had always been the case. Still, from the banter of some of her more talkative customers, she knew the route was being built well west of her.

"I have no idea how close I'll be to the highway."

faintly, a hint of laughter even as the door to the Fox closed behind her. Who would want to know such things? She stood in the early evening of Bakersfield, the street lined up and down with the other patrons' cars ready to take them home.

What a change—to go from the dread of being talked about as the mother of Dan Watson to stupidly wondering if the young people in town would think of her as a woman offended by a film, stomping out in indignation.

She went to work the next day and faced her usual stoic customers, looking for some sign that one of their sons or daughters might have mentioned seeing her at the picture house, but no one said a word. She set late-breakfast plates in front of Vernon and Cal as she always had. None of the young waitresses asked if she'd seen any films lately. No one said a thing.

All the days could do, she realized, was roll along. For all her shame in admitting that the spectacle on the screen had embarrassed her, no one actually cared. She was nothing but a shadow in the dark.

Over at the girl's apartment, no other cheap bouquets ever showed up, and she began to wonder if there might even be another story attached to the one she had seen. Maybe it hadn't even been left in memory, but was the remnant of a date gone wrong, some young people at the bowling alley, perhaps.

August passed. The fall came, with the light softening in the window. December rolled past, and with it the first anniversary of that young girl's death, but no one looked at Arlene in silent knowing. Not the other waitresses, not Vernon, not Cal, not that young deputy who would come in for a grilled cheese, home fries, and a cola.

People were going to forget that girl, Arlene realized. Just as they were beginning to forget her—Arlene Watson.

The days kept going. She spread the news of the world on the café counter and watched the stories swallow up her hands, ink all over her fingertips. The light stung in the windows again, announcing spring, anticipating summer.

"Has anyone come to see you about your motel, Mrs. Watson?" Cal asked.

It was July. It was 1961. She looked up at Cal.

"You've been asking me that question for years, Cal."

"The planning is over," he said, pointing to the newspaper. "They're building."

She had known they were. She didn't let on that she had stood on the edge of the motel parking lot, shading her eyes west. Past the fiery line of sunset, she could see nothing but empty space there, a horizon pulled taut. She didn't know what she had expected to see—cranes, maybe, or the elevated ramps and thick pillars of highways like she had seen on television.

"Why would they come see me?"

"Are they anywhere close to your property? Could they buy you out?"

There hadn't been much letup in her motel bookings. Sometimes weekends were slow, but that had always been the case. Still, from the banter of some of her more talkative customers, she knew the route was being built well west of her.

"I have no idea how close I'll be to the highway."

"It's a freeway, not a highway," said Vernon.

"Freeway or highway, what's the difference?" she asked.

"We already have a highway," said Vernon. "That's the problem." He sopped at his eggs over easy with a piece of bread and grabbed his silverware to demonstrate. "See these two lanes?" He placed the fork and knife next to each other. "They're going in the same direction. There's two other lanes right next to them going in the opposite direction. Just like the highway we have now." He hovered his hand over the silverware, as if it were a car traveling. "Problem right now is that we run right through Bakersfield and Tulare and Kingsburg and so forth. The city traffic slows for all sorts of reasons. Stop signs or speed limits or cars pulling into motel parking lots." Vernon motioned his hovering hand slowly to the right of the silverware. "With the new freeway, you don't have none of that. Just a straight shot through. You get on by a ramp and you get off by a ramp. Easy breezy. No stop signs, nothing to slow the traffic down."

"So?" she asked. "How's that different?"

"Come on, Mrs. Watson," said Cal. "Don't tell me you can't do the math. If I'm paying a trucker to get a load of eggs to Sacramento, do I want him there in five hours or seven? He could do five on the freeway because he never, ever has to stop or slow down. Unless he wants a cup of coffee." He held out his cup. "That's a different story."

She poured, and Vernon finished with the silverware demonstration, taking them back up once again for his breakfast. "I hate to say it, but Cal was right all along. You should start thinking about selling that motel if you can."

"No, Vernon, I can't let that go."

"Darlin'," he said, putting down his utensils, "you're just not going to have people stopping at the motel anymore. Not unless one of those ramps is close by."

"People will still use the old Ninety-nine. Why wouldn't they? You don't just tear up a road that goes through town."

"Arlene, you want to see it? You want to see the freeway with your own eyes?" Vernon asked. "What time do you get off shift today? I'll drive you out there myself."

"I get off at three."

"I'll be here."

That afternoon, Vernon followed her to the motel. He drove a brand-new truck, sturdy and somehow elegant for its size and what he used it for. Vernon, she knew, was the kind of man who kept his possessions meticulously clean. She regretted that it was a Tuesday—the motel parking lot sat empty for lack of customers, and she hated for Vernon to see this. Arlene hurried from her vehicle with keys in hand, if only to keep Vernon from surveying the scene and saying something about her spotty business.

His truck was comfortable and the ride smooth. The air conditioner was on low, but the cab felt almost cold. "I've been watching them start on this thing for years. Just bit by bit. And they've got people working from here all the way up through Sacramento."

"That's good work, I guess," Arlene said. "There's always people looking for a job around here." She looked out at the fields rolling by, and for the first time in a while, she thought of her older brother.

"I knew your husband, Frederick, a little bit," said Vernon. He cleared his throat.

"How so?" She knew this but, surprised that Vernon had mentioned Frederick, put up a pretense.

"In town. You know how it is. Good people."

The truck hummed along and Arlene waited for him to continue. She realized, too late, that she hadn't said anything in agreement.

"I think he would've wanted you to sell that motel," he said.

"He ain't dead, Vernon," she said. "He left me."

"Arlene, he'd want you—"

"I could give a good goddamn what he would've wanted me to do."

Vernon pursed his lips a bit. "What I mean . . . what's best for you . . ." That didn't sound right either and he stopped with a brief sigh. "It's just a bad decision to hang on to that place, Arlene. Believe me. I've got property. You might end up with taxes on a place you can't afford if the money stops flowing in. That's all I'm saying."

Up ahead, finally, she could see how the landscape had changed. Up ahead, she could see what it meant when Vernon said "ramp." The road elevated in the distance.

"See that?" he said. "That's the freeway."

He slowed to a crawl and then turned the truck onto a dirt lane bordering a vineyard. The bumpy lane paralleled the new freeway, a deep ravine and fencing separating it from the site. Vernon guided the truck among the holes and the kicking dust and then finally stopped. "There it is."

The two lanes shot north. The pavement seemed to glisten in the afternoon sun, a fresh gray, free of oil or grit, almost reflective in its newness. The lanes spanned wide, with generous shoulder room on either side, and even though Arlene could see enormous mounds of earth and gaps in the pavement only several feet away, it was clear that the freeway was a progression unimpeded. Up ahead, she could see the beginnings of a ramp and a completed overpass.

"Ah, that," said Vernon. He eased the pickup truck along the dirt lane as far as the property line allowed, and Arlene could see why he had driven that distance. An enormous green sign loomed: UNION AVENUE.

"That's the exit?"

"Straight into town," said Vernon. "That means if someone takes that off-ramp and is looking for a place to sleep, your motel will already be behind them."

The truck was still running, the air conditioner going at its low hum, still cold. Even so, Arlene could feel the sweat beginning to stick to the back of her waitress uniform. They sat in silence for a while, Vernon not turning off the truck.

Finally, Arlene shook her head slowly. "I wouldn't know how to handle all that . . . paperwork . . . and . . . well . . ."

"You need to do it, though," said Vernon, and he reached over and set his hand on top of hers. His hand was enormous and she could feel the calluses on his palms from his hard work. It was sweaty from having held the steering wheel. His hand did not move and neither did his fingers, and Arlene's heart beat fast at his gesture. She waited for him to say something, maybe something about Frederick, what a fool he had been, but Vernon said nothing, and for a moment, Arlene wondered if his hand was nothing more than reassurance, that he recognized the gravity of her situation more than she did. When this thought crossed her mind, Arlene found herself oddly moved, and she felt tears coming, a knot in her throat. She swallowed hard to keep from crying.

Vernon moved his hand to her knee.

She pulled away as if touched by fire. "Vernon . . . ," she said.

"Arlene, I just want you to know . . ."

"Take me home," she said. "Please."

What she had wanted was a quick drive home, but instead she had to endure the slow ease of the dirt lane all the way out to the main road. Their silence deepened and she kept expecting Vernon to offer a measure of apology. He stayed quiet, and Arlene felt the tears form and fall. She had no choice but to wipe at her cheeks and she turned away to the side window to do so, but she knew Vernon had seen her.

"I'm real sorry, Arlene . . . ," Vernon began when he had pulled his pickup to a stop back at the motel parking lot, but by that time, Arlene had already opened the door to the truck cab and jumped out. She hurried to the house, listening for Vernon's truck to gear. It finally did as her hands shook, trying to get the key into her front door lock.

She felt deeply shamed for the rest of the afternoon. That's what the feeling was, in the end, a deep shame. Arlene could not identify what it was about Vernon or his gesture or her tears that prevented her from touching her dinner that evening, that kept her with her eyes open all night, lying in bed with her hands involuntarily smoothing her stomach, as if she were trying to keep something from rising. Whatever it was, though, felt exactly like all of those afternoons in the first months after Dan had disappeared, the eyes in the café silently watching her, felt exactly like the moment she had moved through the darkness of the picture house, her shadow laughable in its anonymous anger. She was no one that anyone had to worry about, and to think that someone like Vernon might ever have held feelings for her. What a fool not to have seen it, not to have believed it. All this time, she had been thinking of herself in the way others saw her—an abandoned wife, a lowly waitress, an aging woman whom no one could even bother to gossip about anymore—but Vernon himself had not.

The next morning, she rose with a bleary resolution to apologize to Vernon, somehow send him a sign that she, in fact, understood what he was offering, that his gesture was not unlike the shine of the camera bulbs in the movie magazines, a promise of a different life altogether. He had her best interests in mind, saw her as belonging in another space, not the motel, maybe not even the café.

But Vernon did not come in for his usual breakfast, Cal sitting alone with his newspaper. The next morning, he did not come either. Cal made no mention of Vernon's absence and she was too embarrassed to pose an innocent question to him about Vernon's whereabouts, to ask if Vernon had taken ill. Arlene let the anticipation sit. The small dot within her knew better. It knew in the same way she knew something when she stepped out of the picture house, when she saw the taillights of Dan's escape, when she rested her head on Frederick's chest on their wedding night, when she spotted her brother on the road, years and years and years ago.

Things change, the small dot told her. But she was not going to be able to.

This was July 1961. Vernon never came into the café again. That fall, Cal married a clerk from the shoe store, and the two had a baby, and the farmers who came in to fill where Vernon and Cal had once sat were not much interested in either Arlene or her daily newspaper reading, the outside world being something they would rather not deal with.

She wished now that she could remember the day—the exact day—when she stopped looking at the café door in anticipation. The day she stopped waiting for a policeman to come in to report on Dan, Vernon to come in with his hat in his hands. Time just passed.

It took a year from that moment for the freeway to open, in summer 1962.

Talk around the café was about the boom in business along Union Avenue. The freeway fed the street like a vein with Los Angeles traffic. The café bustled, but her motel vacancy rate jumped, more than half the rooms empty, some weekends without a single customer at all. When Arlene began to recognize a set of regulars—truckers who went all the way north to Oregon and Washington State—she suspected that many of them stopped not only out of loyalty and familiarity but out of a bit of pity as well.

She watched as Union Avenue underwent construction to accommodate the new traffic, the buzz in downtown all about the flood of anticipated business. Construction crews busied themselves with roof work, facade restructurings, paint jobs, drills busting up the concrete sidewalks. Arlene wasn't fooled by any of it. The small dot inside her told her to watch the condition of the vinyl seating in the café, the minuscule rips becoming long, jagged tears. It told her to watch as the summer season went by and the owner neglected to freshen up the paint. It told her to watch as the pedestrian traffic began to lessen, the cars inching along the street to the far end, where the town had been dazzled by the newer strip malls and a Texaco gas station selling hot dogs. She kept putting breakfast plates on the table, but now news was about heart attacks and strokes, her sturdy men not doing well in the heat like they used to. The tips got smaller, the hands holding the coins a little sheepish about what they were able to put down. She felt the café slip right through the town's fingers, the way it stopped being the center of anything, and out in the world, the Cubans threatened, but the small dot within her confirmed that this was the inevitability of all things. The world meant nothing because this was the life she had chosen, this space with plate-glass windows from floor to ceiling, which looked more shoddy by the year.

The president was shot and killed in Dallas and the girls in the kitchen hovered around the TV set, their hands on the antenna to bring in the hazy news. The motel got so bad that Arlene took to letting out some of the rooms at the far end to the café girls who got in trouble with a baby but had no man around. The Los Angeles paper gave her news of the boiling race relations in the South. She had dreams of Kennedy, the president smiling at her with enormous, bloody teeth. Slowly, the familiar faces of the farmers began to disappear, more and more of them.

Things change, but she wasn't ever going to.

Around town, she was known as just Arlene after all.

When she looked up from the counter, eyes away from the newspaper, it was another year gone, another time coming, the light in the café window sometimes blunt, sometimes wavering, but she was powerless to ever make it appear otherwise.

That was exactly how the years were going to race, now that she had nothing.

You can't go back in, ma'am—the voice of the theater concession clerk coming back to mock her.

When she looked up from the counter, it was 1968 and she was fifty-six years old. It was as if she'd never been anybody's anything.

"Arlene," said one of the girls during a break. She was the youngest sibling of one of the girls Arlene used to supervise, years ago, but now here was proof yet again of change. Her name was Peggy.

"Are you going to watch Petula Clark next week?" Peggy asked. "Do you like her?" She pointed to a picture in the newspaper.

"I do, actually," Arlene replied. She peered down to the newspaper and followed the girl's finger to the article.

"It says they might not air her special because she touched a black man," the girl said, her voice a little louder than it needed to be, gleeful at how she'd caused the slight head raises from some of the older farmers.

"Oh, now . . ." Arlene began to read the article. "It's Harry Belafonte."

"So why is it such a big deal?"

"You know how people are," Arlene said, but she read the rest of the article, which told her about local affiliates being left to choose whether to broadcast the event. Inside, she held a quiver of disbelief and anticipation over how angry the show

sponsors had been about Petula Clark touching Harry Belafonte, the fine line being walked. What kind of touching was it,
these two being so harmless? She continued through the rest
of the article and then handed the newspaper back to the girl.
"That's some stuff."

"Do you think our affiliate will carry it?"

"Of course they will. LA is right over the hill." She said it as
if she traveled right over the Grapevine all the time, as if she
knew all about places like Los Angeles and how the big cities
had been facing these years of change.

The only time she'd ever been out of Bakersfield was for her
honeymoon drive to the coast with Frederick to see the big
rock sitting in the middle of Morro Bay.

For the rest of the afternoon, she couldn't get Petula Clark's
"Downtown" out of her head despite the café's constant music.
She smiled to herself at the song's foolishness, thinking of Bakersfield's broad, desolate avenues, its languishing TG&Y with
the empty parking lot, its forlorn flower shop across the street.
She shook her head at the thought of how much she had liked
the song not that long ago, how'd she thought of the song's
promise and invitation. *Dreaming just like my young girls,* she
thought, picturing them awkward with a tray of drinks, the way
they flirted with the men their age, what they were imagining
for a future. It dawned on her that Petula Clark must've been
singing of some place she had been enraptured by. Enough to
write a song about it. Enough to put to words how the act of
going to that place lifted her spirits.

Bakersfield was nothing to sing about.

When the Petula Clark show came on the air, it was the first week of April. The weather was warm. She left the front door open so she could hear any trucks pull into the motel parking lot—she didn't want to have to rise from her chair once the show started. Petula Clark appeared and sang a handful of songs that Arlene vaguely remembered, others she'd never heard at all. The hour ticked by, but still no Harry Belafonte. The parking lot stayed silent. Finally, he loomed on the screen after a commercial break, Petula Clark in the distance, as if wondering whether to approach him. He began to sing in his delicious voice, and she walked toward him, closer and closer, until she stood by him. The paper said that Petula Clark would touch a black man and wondered openly about an uproar in the South, maybe even in other places throughout the United States. Arlene waited for the moment, almost holding her breath.

Quietly, without much fanfare, Petula Clark rested her hand on Harry Belafonte's arm. She rested it as if she needed to steady herself. Both of them were wearing white clothing: he in a tucked-in sweater and trousers, she in an elegant and tasteful dress. Maybe the clothing was cream-colored—Arlene couldn't tell because of the fading picture quality of her television set. They sang the rest of the song with Petula's hand on Harry Belafonte's arm, and Arlene heard no murmur of audience disapproval. Then she remembered it had been taped to begin with, not live, not an audience watching them. She imagined people in the South turning off their sets, if they had bothered to watch at all. But she knew they watched. It had been all over the news, how a man and a woman who shouldn't touch were going to do so. The newspaper didn't say how they touched, and that was why everyone needed to see it. To see just how much things were changing.

So much time had passed, so many years. And just how were things really changing? She worked in a café that had nowhere to go but into decline. The motel, in the end, was housing a pregnant girl or two, and there wasn't much she could ever hope for in selling it.

The program ended. Petula Clark did not sing "Downtown," but Arlene heard a riff of it near the finish. Outside, the parking lot remained quiet. There would be no one coming tonight. When the credits finished rolling, Arlene debated watching the next program to lull her to sleep, but instead she got up from the chair and turned off the TV. She walked out to the porch. She thought of her days as a little girl. All these years. She was fifty-six years old. She put her hand on her elbow, resting it there the way Petula Clark had touched Harry Belafonte. The gesture had meant nothing more than kindness. The gesture reminded her of Vernon, how long it had been now since she'd seen him, and of all the regrets in her life, this was the one that stung the most.

It was all hers, all private, the one thing that no one else had witnessed, all hers to embrace. She knew Vernon would never have spoken about it. His hand on her hand, then on her knee, the calluses, what a hard worker he was. All those years, he'd been a very kind customer, seated at the counter with a comforting regularity. He had meant well by her. He could have spared her what was coming. He'd been a very decent man, but it was too late, too late. She was standing on a dark porch, just as she had been years ago, waiting for her brother. She tried to think back to the day when everything—everything, everything—had gone wrong, to the day that had led to this moment, but she couldn't see it. She looked as hard as she could into the dark but she couldn't see it.

Eleven

H e settled into his seat and readied for the journey back. His wife read one of the magazines, the type too small for his comfort. The Director was flying back to Los Angeles after a triumph long in coming. He would never admit such a thing to many around him, but he had missed the dazzle of the red carpet: the jewels parading on by, each piece bigger and more expensive than the last, borrowed emeralds nestled on top of a starlet's breasts. How was it possible that the starlets got more and more beautiful every year? Daffodil chiffon, green silk, a leopard-print shawl. Handsome men in bow ties too uncomfortable after four whiskeys, and the flashbulbs now just a continuous silent sprinkling of light. He missed the old days, the actual pop of the cameras, and the patience of the women making entrances, waiting for the polite photographers to ready themselves, holding their poses as the magazines did the important work of capturing the women's evening wear. No longer. It was 1972. Everything was much faster, the cameras mirroring exactly what the films themselves had been doing: less posture and key lighting, more spontaneity and room for the everyday flaw, with anything beautiful rising straight to the surface.

In Cannes, though, he had mostly stood away from the evening red carpets and the buzz of the cameras and had gone, instead, to the morning cafés with their cigarette smoke and their folded newspapers, the magazine writers nursing gin-and-tonic hangovers, readying for their day's scheduled viewings. The Director could take very little of the pretensions aired at the evening parties, the mood tight with apprehension and handshakes, who was meeting whom. Evenings brought affect, good impressions, boisterous grace, and big smiles, all lining up for another film deal, a possible magazine article, a job. Mornings, though, brought what the Director enjoyed: the quiet, studious cafés adjacent to the hotels, where the cinema writers in their dark glasses clearly recognized him but left him alone to enjoy the windows open to the sea air drifting in. In the morning came the world newspapers, heavy with the reviews of the festival's previous evening's screenings, and he enjoyed eavesdropping on those who had a good handle on French or German as they rustled through all the reviews for comparison. He could spend the entire morning there without saying a word, no one disturbing him, eyes on his own newspaper, pretending to read but enjoying the two loud British journalists in the corner disagreeing with a review in *Le Soir*, their tones as surly as the publication's, both of them with fixed ideas of cinema and no room for change.

The Director was grateful for any morning without intrusion, and on days when a cinephile—always a young man— dared to approach his table, he managed to dissuade him with a sharp, arched look of disapproval. The young men came, like they all did, hoping for a chance to talk to him about the Great Art, but the truth was, he was rarely in much of a mood for such conversations. He was nearing, he knew, the end of a very long career, and his own embrace of change had slowed, his ideas fixed, the difficulty of a new creation more and more daunting. In America, change had come rapidly after the demise of the old penny-pinching studio heads. Too much had changed for those studio heads to follow only their old ways about story and the traditional three-arc narrative. Now there was color to worry about, and saturation to master, and sound overlap to toy with, as well as 65-millimeter handheld cameras, and antireflective optical lenses, and helicopter shots, and automatic zooms—too many tools for even someone like him to get a handle on, to investigate their best uses. And, certainly, too many young mavericks with the willingness to not only try them out but master them, use the tools alone or together in the service of a story that was beyond what had once been acceptable. Things were changing. The old stories seemed like lazy standbys: pickup scripts from the better Broadway shows, or the more successful novels, or the particularly strange human-interest story glanced at by chance in a newspaper during a transatlantic flight just like this one.

When the plane was airborne, the Director settled back into his seat and closed his eyes, trying to sleep. He needed rest after the excitement of his moderate success. A return to form, it was being called, and he tried not to make much of some of the morning articles he'd read, croissant in hand, that stated it was his first unqualified success in twelve years. Twelve years!

Unqualified! He'd done several pictures since then, some television, the money pouring in because of his shrewd handling. He didn't like this tone, the implied judgment, but he knew its root. What he had accomplished twelve years earlier with a motel shower had been simultaneously a high and a low, both what he could never surpass and what others imitated, a distinct point in the history of the entire form. There, twelve years ago, was a marker. There was the new violence. There was the door to the unthinkable. There was the door to the unmentionable.

To be fair, this was said all the time. Five years ago, the handsome Warren Beatty had traded in his own shiny stardom for the crude mask of a criminal, shooting his way into the psyche of an audience who had forever wanted him in only minor variations of the cad, the suave suitor. A year later, Frank Sinatra's wife cut off all of her hair and headlined as a woman raped by Satan himself. Someone had the nerve to show full blood in the chaos of a gangster shoot-out! Someone had the nerve to show the devil's eyes! The line could be pushed forward without end, what the human eye could possibly witness without turning away, and already he felt far away from the moment when he had made such a mark. Could he ever make one again?

There was going to be an end point to all these visual highbars. The Americans—they always crossed the line, not knowing when to stop. They saw no poetry in taking the strange road into the desert, hesitating to go any further. The Director recalled talks in the French cafés about Rossellini and how the Americans devoured the man's personal indiscretions with Ingrid Bergman, as if the man had never captured the city of

Rome at its most desolate and crumbling, his camera swooping into place to order all the chaos with nothing but the vigor of story. Could the Americans ever have pulled off that kind of realism? Could they have offered an elegant answer to Anna Magnani's frantic run in the street, chasing the military truck that had carted off her fiancé, her arm raised in a futile gesture to halt? The Americans didn't have an actress who could have tumbled in the street at the sound of machine-gun fire. They had body doubles to save the million-dollar legs.

The Director was heading home to Los Angeles, but he knew that once he returned to the States, the great glow of this recent public appearance would quickly fade. The Americans looked at nothing but surface. He had no big stars this time around, his radiant blonds not in place. What would the Americans do with nothing glamorous to look at? This was why they were so good at those CinemaScope films, made to combat the lure of the home television sets, even if the screen held only wide, long landscape shots without a human being in sight. The Americans were good at lineups of Broadway dancers with legs kicking across the screen. They were exceptional at Bible stories acted out in tony British accents and couture costumes, or star vehicles with exquisite set design but not much of a script. They were good at hookers with hearts of gold. They were good at buckshot violence and bullet sprays, two-bit actors falling in familiar agony. At one time, even the Director would admit, they had been the best at women's pictures, never enough ways for a woman to quiver at the hell of keeping the secret of an illegitimate child close to her heart, all the while weeping.

The problem with the Americans was that they had had no

idea what to do with the violence since he'd given them permission, in his mind, to start filming it with his own bravura
take, twelve years earlier. The Americans were always good at
dying, but not death. Good at plot, but not fatalism. Good at
cowboys shot down from the backs of horses, but not the final-
ity of writhing in the dust. Good at the cars roaring lustily into
each other as if no one were in them, but not the full horror of
a body hurtling into the rigidity of the steering column. Good
at the beautiful Radcliffe heroine succumbing to cancer in her
bed, but not the ugly business of the night nurse wiping her
clean at two in the morning.

What they didn't know was that you take the little glimmer
of the truth of death when you see it, and then have the nerve
to give it light.

Like Gene Hackman being lured into the dark, dangerous
silence of an abandoned warehouse, gun drawn in both fear and
stubborn will, and the audience left in unfulfilled suspense.

Like the dance marathon contestant, played by Jane Fonda,
shot in the head while standing on a California pier, yet falling
in a field of tall grass.

Like the wondrous Altman western, with Warren Beatty
again, the outlaw fatally wounded in the deepening snow.

Or like the Coppola picture he'd screened only two months
ago, a man shot bullet dead center in the head, the bullet con-
tinuing its travel to shatter the window in the background. As
real bullets must, the force they carry not to be impeded.

He'd seen how an audience rustled in the dark when they responded to a moment like this. He liked the feeling of unease,
of excitement, of repulsion, the terrific jolt he received from

knowing he had created an image that provoked people. In this film, he knew he had such a sequence. But even he had been astounded by the response.

The film had been slated to screen out of competition. The Director had, at most, modest expectations. The setting was not America, but London. There were no American stars, only Brits. The film had a washed-out color to it, an unfamiliarity. Gone were the actresses with the stylized wardrobes. Gone were the actresses as gorgeous centerpieces. Gone were the days when he could get away with suggesting the menace of violence. Now everyone had to see it. He was over seventy years old, and some people in the audience thought the Director had lost his sure hand when they witnessed the vulgarity of a rape, the pink bud of a nipple being loosened from behind a bra cup. They sat in silence as the killer removed his necktie to strangle his victim. That would have been enough in the old days, the hand on the necktie, the audience already aware that a man was wandering the streets of London strangling women. But this was no longer the old days. Some people groaned at the extended scene of the woman's struggle, her fingers panicked at the tightening around her neck. Some people groaned at its excess. Some people groaned at the time in which they were all living, how even someone like the Director had little choice but to cave in to such unthinkable images. A woman's violated breast. A stretch of spittle from a dead woman's gaping mouth.

But later in the film, something different happened. Another death was coming. The audience knew. There was no suspense. It was coming, like seeing two cars careering into an intersection with no way for either to slow down. There she was, the woman. By this point, the audience knew what women were for. She wore an ordinary dress, orange with white buttons, nothing glamorous like the one some people in the audience remembered Grace Kelly wearing—ice blue satin. She carried a white bag and stormed out of a pub, only to be met unexpectedly by the killer. He was a charmer. They walked together through the bustle of Covent Garden, passersby hauling flowers and sacks of vegetables. The killer lured her easily to his flat. They walked there together. They climbed the red-carpeted stairs, her white shoes and the give of the carpet. The audience knew what was going to happen in that room, but the camera stopped on the landing. It stopped on the landing and watched the woman enter, the killer following behind. The camera did not move. The audience noticed. The camera stayed as if to watch, then began a slow reversal down the steps. The camera looked away from the door. The camera caught the deep red floral pattern of the cheap curtains on the landing window. It caught the zigzag of the fire escape of the building across the way. It caught the quiet of the stairwell, no one hearing what was going on upstairs. It caught the gradual descent into the empty, lonely hallway, then the slow exit to the street, to the bustle of the everyday, the trundling wheelbarrows, the footsteps, the trucks loaded with produce, the vegetable sacks being lugged over shoulders, the street so noisy and the window up above where everything terrible was happening but need not be shown.

In his airplane seat, the Director floated halfway between a mild nap and the fluttering of his eyes, fully awake to the world, but he remained in the magic of the audience's response to the long sequence, a standing ovation right in the middle of his film. All the papers made mention of the moment. They cheered his restraint, his elegant answer to prurience, as much as they cheered his return, as if acknowledging how much they'd taken for granted his enormous skill and grandeur, the great pleasure he had given them. Back in the world of the airplane, the lights low, his wife turning the pages of her magazine, his mind refused to leave that space where the applause deafened and would not yield, and he let himself drown in the cascade of acclaim. There was no star in the sequence, no blond arching to reach for a pair of scissors, no blond in a fitted pea green jacket fending off an attack of crows. Just the camera on the landing. Just him.

He opened his eyes for a moment and caught the stewardess in first class observing him. Her eyes made as if to shift away, but then she moved forward, smiling, as if to check whether he needed something. He needed nothing. He closed his eyes once more, and soon enough he was back in the audience, enjoying its echo, the shouts of approval, the keen embrace of complete adoration.

Twelve

The ring on your finger means a beginning is coming, but also an end. This is the aim in this town, to get a ring on the finger, to be ushered past the white fence and the rich red roses, to be pulled out of the rain. To step into a church and then step out of it, back out into the Bakersfield sunshine, but not alone, and all around are people who have joined themselves to others in the same way. The ring means you'll be a wife, and the clean-cut boy who presented it has already promised you will no longer have to work in the shoe store. A beginning, but an end. No more toiling for Mr. Carson, no more long hours in the hot stuffiness of the store's back room. A wife need not work. A wife gets a bouquet of promises: devotion, security, honor, hard work from her husband's hands. The clean-cut boy wants no wife of his working, and this satisfies you. You have deserved this all along.

But the ring also means no more being the center. No more being able to lean toward the women patrons when they come not to try on shoes but to gossip, to let you in on whatever rumor floats around town.

In December, in early January, after the girl was murdered, the clientele had come in droves. Mr. Carson had pursed his lips at the women who arrived in the shop, who hardly even glanced at the merchandise, didn't even bother to pretend. He stuffed his face with danish to keep himself from speaking out, not wanting to chastise his best customers at the height of the holiday buying season, but he bristled at the same thing you bristled at: the lack of decorum in these ladies, their visible thirst for word about that girl, the way they looked at the heavy curtain leading to the back room of the shop, as if tracing her steps would tell them everything they wanted to know about her. You wanted to point out the inexpensive black flats that the girl liked to wear—*These, right here,* you wanted to tell them— knowing the ladies in the group would feel a proximity to that girl just by the weight of her shoes, the smallest detail budding into significance.

But what could you have said to them? What did you know? You saw nothing. You weren't there. You weren't in her shoes.

"She was such a quiet girl," you told them. This was true, but you didn't want to tell them much more than that.

The ladies all knew about Dan Watson. Their feigned expressions of surprise didn't convince you. They knew his mother from the town café, but his mother wasn't in his swagger. His good mother wasn't in the way he stepped out of his truck, cocked his hips as he lit a cigarette, waiting to cross the street. You know they had all looked at him with longing. He was no clean-cut boy like your soon-to-be husband, no straight line across the back of his neck from a dutiful Monday-morning haircut.

Actions like that should surprise no one. All around town, if people had only put their heads together, done the hard work of separating rumor from truth, of confirming what had been seen and not heard, nothing should have surprised anyone.

You didn't tell these ladies much, no, not in December in the early days of the shock, and not in January, when it felt as if it might be best to toss out an observation, like a coin into a pool of water, just to see the ripples. But then the ring changed everything, and with it came a promise that you would be able to put all such ugliness to rest, never again having to step into Mr. Carson's store, not one more reminder of that girl, living and breathing as she once was, coming around to haunt you. Marriage was coming for you, and with it would come a startling privacy, you nested in your brand-new home, guarding the things you learned about the family you would be married into: your husband-to-be the middle brother of three boys, the other two living in suspicious bachelorhood.

Marriage was going to save you from having to say anything at all to these ladies. You didn't tell them about the last time you had been escorted to Las Cuatro Copas, your boyfriend eager to see what all the fuss had been about, those illustrations in the town newspaper and the drive-in shut down for the winter. If the murder hadn't happened, perhaps you would've been able to make small talk about the crudeness of the cantina, the unsavory mixing of whites and Mexicans and how maybe Bakersfield shouldn't be allowing such a thing. Or maybe you would've complimented the cheap but delicious taquitos served up by that girl, who looked only at your boyfriend, not willing to look you in the eye, not willing to acknowledge that she needed another job, that she even knew you. But you wouldn't tell the women that—you'd tell them only about the cheap food, point to this as perhaps one of the reasons the night was such a weekly success. None of you would admit that it was really about Dan Watson up onstage. None of you would admit that it was the way that girl sang, the way her head turned to look at Dan Watson while she held a long note. The little storm he created inside her pushed to get out: you could all see it, how he was teaching her to sing, to let go of whatever caught in her throat. He shaped the thrust of her shoulder when she stood sideways to the audience, hand on the microphone, all those men looking at her. The more she sang, the more comfortable she became with their looking, the more she wanted their looks.

To say you saw this would mean you envied her. To say you saw this would mean you, too, looked at Dan Watson.

That night, there was another man in the back. You could tell by the way that girl brought her voice inward, her eyes squinting as if to confirm what she had recognized, and her easy flirtation with Dan Watson hardened into a forced gesture. Something had changed within her. You turned your head to look back there because you knew she was ashamed—all along she should have been ashamed, the way she held the edge of her baby blue satin cowgirl dress, and those boots. Those boots! You hardly had time to register where you had seen those boots when that look flickered across her face, and you turned to study who was in the back, which face was going to shimmer into the person who could make her so apprehensive. Back there, though, stood a line of short Mexican men with no dates, hands in their pockets, their white T-shirts gleaming through the cigarette smoke.

You don't tell the ladies any of this because you don't know where to start. She wore boots she'd stolen from Mr. Carson, but what did that fact say about her murder? A line of short Mexican men stared at her through the smoke, but what did that say about the one the police ended up deporting?

Or this: A few days later, on a Monday, as you stepped out of the shop's back room into the dusty alley out back, a little jar sitting on top of the garbage can. At first you thought it was from your clean-cut boyfriend, the jar sealed tight, with its label removed, and but inside lay a card from the Mexican bingo game, tilted to the side. A picture of a rose. Such specificity! Such imagination! LA ROSA and the number 41. Not your language. Colors in the faded scheme of the Mexican restaurant on the corner, that dusty blue, that exhausted pink. The gift was for that girl, but you crammed the jar into your purse as you scanned the empty alley. Around the corner, you tossed it into one of the city's corner trash bins.

You don't tell the ladies about that. What would this fact mean? What is the fact? That there was a jar? Or that the girl never received it?

Another jar appeared, its Gerber baby-food label missing and inside a store of shelled walnuts. The only reason you didn't take it was the dark shape of a head ducking around the building at the end of the alley, studying, watching, guarding. Off you went, as you always would, rounding the corner, and just a ways down stood a short Mexican man in a white T-shirt, everything about his slender body tight and worked, as if he'd gathered those walnuts himself, up in Pixley in the center of the Valley, where the harvest had been going on, and when you passed him—this Mexican man who had no business just standing on a street corner like that—you understood that something had gone on between him and that girl, something Dan Watson didn't know about, something that girl had held close to her when she measured the sultriness of her singing.

These are facts. Everyone in town has facts. They bring them out into the open to give them sense, even when there is none to be made. But you saw it. You put it all together.

That night, the girl held a hand at her throat, as if the thick cotton of a cold was catching. She had begged off singing. The crowd had been disappointed when Dan Watson made the announcement, but they lured her onstage with determined applause. She sang a Patsy Cline number very poorly, and even though she was showered with polite clapping, she made a funny grimace and gestured at her throat. The crowd allowed her offstage without much protest, and Dan Watson had to sing alone. She had stepped back behind the bar to watch him. Everyone watched him. You watched him. The hard stare of that man hiding in the shadows watched him. Dan Watson took command of the stage in his dark jeans and boots, a white cowboy hat still on. His body stood still—hips, upper body, even his knees refusing to quiver with nerves—and he announced that he would be doing an old Carl Smith song, "Hey Joe!" He held the guitar firmly and then began, all eyes on the quick dancing of his right hand, the song jumpy and energetic, a song about making his attentions clear to steal a friend's girl.

She had watched him, his stiff, hard body, the white hat

casting a shadow over his eyes, over half of his face, so that all the women in the audience could look only at his hard mouth.

That girl had been jealous, knowing those women had looked at Dan like that.

You had looked at Dan Watson like that.

That nameless Mexican face along the back wall must have seethed at how the women looked at Dan, the ripple of need he set off in them, sitting next to their clean-cut men.

All that need. Husbands fail. Boyfriends cannot provide. Men in the cantina feeling they could never match up against someone like Dan Watson, the collapsing darkness of the place allowing them to hide that fear. Whoever that Mexican face belonged to, nothing he could ever do would match whatever Dan Watson offered her.

Not a week later came the night in question.

That girl looking up at the painted ceiling of the Fox Theater, up at every tiny light shining down on her, the ceiling painted dark and swirled with faint clouds, studded with tiny lights that beamed down like stars. She looked up at the painted sky as if Dan Watson had offered it to her himself, as if he were the one who opened the barely contained promise of the Fox Theater in daytime: the scrolls of neon piping, the gallery of lightbulbs waiting to burst bright once the sun went down. All around them, people chose seats without a fuss, but that girl kept looking up in wonder. You knew without knowing that on her lunch breaks she'd gone down to the theater just as she'd gone to the record shop, to peek through the shut doors for the red carpet inside, the velvet ropes hanging on brass stands, the poster images of serious drama, of women in gowns, of love and long looks, of color and intensity, beauty shimmering all around her. She traced the ceiling with her eyes, then followed it all the way down front, where the dark velvet theater ended with an enormous white screen, blank and brilliant with promise.

People milled and chatted, and because it was December, the act of removing a coat gave the men a chance to be gallant, assisting their dates. People got comfortable, the rustle building into the excitement about whatever the screen held in store. This was not the dust and darkness of the drive-in, but the spotlight of standing in queue out front, people showing off their best garments. The women, both the older wives and the younger ones on dates, had arrived in dresses and scarves and earrings. Some of the older men wore hats, which they removed only after they had finally chosen a seat. That girl—what nerve—wore the baby blue satin cowgirl dress with the white fringe from her cantina performances, as if she knew people would recognize her, and you watched as she pretended to fix her hair in the back, the lift of her arm making the fringe on her sleeves dance and sparkle.

The chatter in the theater calmed a bit when the lights dimmed halfway. The gather of smoke from a few cigarettes floated visibly now, but the projector shot out such a bright beam that it hardly mattered. A Looney Tunes cartoon appeared to apparent indifference from the crowd, the last few people scurrying back from the concession stand. More coats removed and draped on the backs of chairs, more people settling in, but when the cartoon ended and the lights went down, the screen went dark, and up came the cheers, the whistles of anticipation.

After all this time, this is the moment you hold and remember, down to the sweaty, nervous palm of your boyfriend: the quiet in the dark of the theater, the story coming.

Darkness used to be the delicious moment of not knowing what would come next. You don't see things like that anymore.

When the light burst on the screen, a desert appeared in a golden hue, a caravan of horses on a winding trail. Your heart sank—a western—but then rose again when the names appeared, one by one, in yellow, rough letters: John Wayne, Dean Martin, Ricky Nelson. His name flashed like an impossible promise. His name flashed as if it had been Dan Watson's, and you read the name with a jealous scan of that girl's head, sitting not four rows ahead of you, how you'd watched her at the record shop that morning, then scurried across the street to see what had captured her attention. Even her obsessions couldn't be your own, Ricky Nelson all hers, and you heard yourself gasp, searching for him in the opening shot of a caravan approaching town, as if seeing him first could give you claim to him. Your eye caught him almost instantly, the cowboy slumped on his horse, looking insolent in his fringed brown suede jacket, his light-colored hat. His name was Colorado, and the caravan leader and John Wayne had a conversation about him that left him unpleased.

"I speak English, Sheriff," he said, "if you want to ask me." His speaking voice sang out just like the one on his records, the ones that girl closed her eyes to in the dark. You closed your eyes, wanting to be like her for a moment, to test whether you could hear his approach like she could, but the possibility of missing that face defeated you. That beautiful face, his lips glistening moist even under the desert sun, his mouth gentle even when it fixed to sing.

All around, some of the younger women rested their heads on the shoulders of their dates. Out of boredom, maybe, especially when Ricky Nelson was not on the screen. Four rows ahead, Dan Watson slipped his arm around that girl, and she tensed, then eased. You tensed, then eased, sensing the heat on the back of your own neck. Some of the younger women drew even closer to their dates, nestling. They didn't care who watched. The married couples sat stiff and proper, two rigid silhouettes. Was marriage love? A wife's shoulders rounded, her body almost curled in, as if protecting the purse in her lap. The young women in the audience ignored John Wayne's gun brandishes and concentrated on the heat near the back of their necks. Dan Watson's arm. Handsome, but not like Ricky Nelson. Rugged and not soft, not moist lipped, not a transfixing star.

Not a whistle-clean Everly Brother either.

If all the women in the audience stared at Ricky Nelson sitting on top of a kitchen table, so did you. Boots resting on a chair, he played guitar for Dean Martin. Your eyes drifted south to his open legs, wanting to study every part of his body, his shape. The theater was dark. This is what people did in the dark. He spoke Spanish, and even that fact—that soft voice saying things you could only dream, candy-sweet and loving—gripped the women in its delicious possibility. That girl knew Spanish. She would know what candy-sweet things he could say. After the first song, Dean Martin ceded the screen to just Ricky, still seated at the table, and all around the theater, women lifted their heads from their dates' shoulders. Ricky alone meant love was coming. Ricky alone meant being torn between the guitar resting on his thigh and the proximity of his long lashes.

The cut of his suede jacket, the dance of its fringe, the round shape of his buttocks when he crossed the room, the angle of his boots on the floor, his youthful face a testament against the coarser ways of older men like John Wayne.

Your boyfriend, your soon-to-be husband, was going to be a John Wayne. You'd already come round to meet the new in-laws, the small, quick-witted mother with the pinched face, the tall father with the gigantic belly, suffering through a forced grapefruit diet. "I have the insides of a steel pipe," he bragged, but in the bathroom of their home, you glimpsed a faint brown smear at the bottom of the toilet.

A vulgar fact. The ugly privacy of marriage.

The two brothers living in suspicious bachelorhood, one going up to San Francisco to live luridly, the other quietly expected to care for their parents once they aged.

Understood facts, no matter that they were vulgar. People said that was what San Francisco was becoming.

So it must be true.

No wonder people applauded the picture when it ended. No wonder they stood up in an excited buzz, the film a respite from their lives, the ugly things they knew. No wonder the crowd took its time to file out of the theater, the house lights brought up, the tiny stars on the ceiling extinguished. Handsome men with mustaches, cowboy hats, shiny belt buckles, all of them walking protectively behind their dates, all of them guarding the women they intended to marry. At the theater, a date was for display. Not like at the drive-in, not like at the grocery store, not like at the café. But eyes everywhere locked on each other in regard, men looking from the safety of where they stood, behind their dates. How many times had men looked at that girl, looked up to see Dan Watson looking back at them, their eyes filled with a different knowing?

Traffic rumbled, headlights all along Union Avenue, as patient as the lines to exit the theater. Some cars drove off toward the Bluebird, toward El Molino Rojo. Married couples drove on to the side streets to their dark homes, the taillights lonely along the road. Everyone else, it seemed, had headed to the Jolly Kone, all the ones in between, too young to be going to the bars so late, too young to be married quite yet.

That was the night in question. People went to the bars to drink or to the Jolly Kone for a burger or right on home. Good married couples went right on home.

None of the ladies who came to the shoe store ever knew about the Jolly Kone. They never knew about the drive-in. The things that went on in both places. You never said a word about the boyfriend taking you there.

The large neon sign lit bright in yellow and blue, an ice cream cone with a grinning, welcoming face. Large orange heaters glowed overhead at the order windows, all the young men with hands in their pockets to keep themselves warm. Dan Watson and that girl had eased right into one of the choice slots, right under the awning near the door.

At the window, a large-breasted teenage girl, blue paper hat pinned in place. She grinned slyly at Dan Watson, her mouth suggesting a banter than involved more than the order. He leaned in, looking up at the posted menu as if he'd forgotten what to say. The waitress stared at his Adam's apple, not minding the wait, but she glanced over at the Ford where that girl sat, as if she'd felt a stern glare coming at her, and the unspoken possession brought her back to jotting in her notepad, closing the window. Dan Watson stood outside under the orange heaters, waiting, and once again it was all there for everyone to see: how steady and strong his back looked, his plaid shirt pressed and tucked in snug at the waist. He was taller than Ricky Nelson, surely, but a survey of the other men milling around, carrying food back to their cars, showed how he stood out. That one was squat and powerful in the legs; another too thin and slender in the chest; yet another had wide, flat buttocks.

Everyone hungry, everyone eating. Dan Watson walking back to the Ford with a box of burgers and greasy fries. The Jolly Kone ice cream sign looked down at everyone with its neon grin.

In the car, your whistle-clean boyfriend pointed to the paper cup of soda lodged between his legs, the two straws poking out of it.

"Thirsty?" he asked.

The pretty, large-breasted waitress shot a stare over at the Ford.

"I'm kidding," he said, but his hand slid over in the shadowy darkness of the car and settled on your knee.

"Not with all these people around," you said.

"Nobody can see," he said, and this was true. People held greasy napkins, sloshed leftover soda; some actually stood outside their cars, necking out in plain view under the yellow and blue sign of the Jolly Kone. Some cars already pulled themselves out of the lot, heading out to the western part of town, to the emptier side, where they could pull into the darkness.

"You getting shy now?"

"Not here."

Not there. You watched the Ford retreat from the front of the Jolly Kone. You watched that girl give one last glare to the pretty waitress as the truck pulled away into the dark. You watched the Ford head back in the direction of that rented room above the bowling alley, the roads considerably cleared, and you could see the truck park in front of the green door leading up to that apartment.

You can see Dan Watson shutting off the engine. You can see the deserted street.

No, you were not there. But you could see it.

And that made it a fact, if you told it.

He stepped out, walking to her side of the truck. He opened her door and held out his hand and she took it. A large, sweaty hand. Strong. Not the hand of someone who could play a guitar softly.

At the shoe store, that girl had always patted her purse as if it contained something secret. Repeatedly. An assurance. What was in there, of course, was her apartment key.

That key slid into the lock of that green door and snapped it open, Dan Watson behind her, his arm above her frame.

The stairwell loomed dark, and what you do with darkness is pitch yourself into it.

So up the stairs they went, her hand fumbling along the wall for the switch but feeling, instead, Dan's strength behind her, his hard torso underneath his shirt.

That night, your boyfriend, your husband-to-be, your clean hairline across the back of the neck, your Everly Brother, walked you to the front door, the light on, the parents sleeping assuredly inside, the porch swing still. At the Jolly Kone, his hand had moved yours to the aching bulge, urging, but marriage was coming. That was not respectable behavior anymore.

You behaved one way at the drive-in, but being a wife means something different. If there's a promise to be a good husband, then the aching bulge can wait until the white fence appears, along with a house with the sparkling kitchen and the shiny teacups.

Up in that room above the bowling alley, she would have tidied up before she left for the theater. What little she had, she had put in its place, no matter that the room looked meager.

A single bed with light blue cotton sheets. A table and a chair. Tin cups, the blue-speckled kind. Blue curtains hanging on a rod.

The blue curtains were a fact. You saw them yourself, fluttering from the window once.

An electric radio? A rotary fan? An iron? The white blouses she wore to work. Her plain black flats. Her blue denim skirt. What else could she have had?

A yellow nightgown, lifted from the top drawer of the dresser, unfurling like a ghost. A patch of white fabric starting at the neckline and covering the breasts, a spring of flowers etched in as decoration.

Like yours.

On the porch, your boyfriend swallowed hard, full of nerve and frustration. You watched his Adam's apple pitch up and down. "Sit with me," he pleaded, pointing to the swing. "I'll be quiet."

What else? Deodorant on top of the dresser and bobby pins and a hairbrush, white cotton panties in the drawer. But toiletries are not possessions, and that girl came from nothing. So she had nothing.

If you bring down those blue curtains, nothing but the cold white light of winter pours in.

"Sit with me," he said.

The way Ricky Nelson had sat on the kitchen table, boots perched on a chair, legs spread wide. Being able to watch him, take him in.

On the porch, you relieve him a bit, touch him. He still doesn't know that he's enormous and beautiful. He won't ever really know, if he keeps the promise of his engagement ring, the metal rubbing him as he closes his eyes.

"You ever think about leaving Bakersfield?"

"Never." That girl says it. The word slips from her because it's true but false at the same time. But it's you who dream of Dan Watson taking you away in his Ford pickup truck, out somewhere to a big white farmhouse with a clothesline out back and a garden and a room where you could watch TV on a set from Stewart's. The word comes from inside, a hesitant, nervous bubble that could not have formed itself fully as a word, and it flashes instead as a smile, her hand moving up to contain it, to hide it. That girl looking down at the floor of her rented room, the rough grain of the wood.

"Closer," he urged.

From the record shop, a collection of A sides, purchased by Dan Watson and handed to her in a brown-papered package: "All I Have to Do Is Dream" by the Everly Brothers. "I Only Have Eyes for You" by the Flamingos. "Put Your Head on My Shoulder" by Paul Anka.

An expensive record player and the needles, too.

"Closer."

The space between is a wide, enormous distance, a destination—there's so much urgency to get across—the pinpoint of some kind of promise way out beyond seeing. Never close enough.

She moved toward him. She moved toward it.

You extended your hand and he reached for it, strong and now clammy with sweat. She raised her hand to his lips very softly, then rested it on his cheek, cupping his face. He kept his hand over yours, moved his fingers across your cheek, your nose, your ears, urging you to touch him. You kissed him and he tasted like cold, like water from a tin cup, the blue-speckled kind.

"Who's Sorry Now?" by Connie Francis. "Tears on My Pillow" by Little Anthony and the Imperials.

He let go of her hands and she could not feel him at all, just her eyes closed to him and his lips wet and cold. She floated, nothing tethering her but Dan Watson's lips, his lips parting and becoming his mouth, the cold giving way to a warmer feel, the dart of his tongue searching her. This was the feeling she liked, his strong hands on her arms, holding her to him, an anticipation, like walking past a flock of birds feeding on street crumbs, waiting for them to burst into the sky at the slightest threatening motion.

"Poor Little Fool" by Ricky Nelson.

Your boyfriend's thigh pressed against yours as you sat on the porch swing, and you wanted to open your eyes to see Dan Watson, his rugged and beautiful face, to see him the way the pretty waitress at the Jolly Kone saw him.

They kept kissing, wet and deep. The bed squeaked. Dan Watson inched closer. She could feel the entire plane of his body now—his leg, his torso, his arm—and she reached down and felt the hard length of him. She kept her hand there, not moving, before giving in to his urgency, his fingers pushing her to explore.

There were men who sat at kitchen tables and sang gentle songs with the round O of their mouths. There were men holding guns, both good and bad. There were men riding sinister horses. There were men hell-bent on terrible missions. There were men who nodded their heads politely at the women. All of them had this need. All of them.

He unbuckled his belt, the sound of the metal unlatching, his jeans undone into a deep V, his underwear pulled down to give a full view. She gripped him harder, enjoying how it forced him to close his eyes, how she'd seen him do this at the drive-in, how she'd done it before. His hands rustled up her skirt and she closed her eyes, how one day they'd do this in their white farmhouse.

You closed your eyes, how one day you'd do this in a white farmhouse.

You could never tell those ladies such a thing.

"That Mexican boy," they said, but they could say nothing more about him.

"I can't imagine . . . ," you said, but you could. That Mexican boy and his gifts in the jar, the way you could feel his hard stare in the darkness of the cantina, the same way you could almost touch the desire of the pretty waitress at the Jolly Kone.

You can imagine.

Maybe an observation, like a coin tossed into a pool of water, just to see the ripples when you tell it.

I heard, you might try, *the Mexican boy showed up that night at her apartment.* People could finish the story with that, jealousy enough of a fuel to explain what happened.

The people in the theater could tell you that men come to blows over women all the time, fists landing in savage anger.

What no longer matters is how Dan Watson killed her. What matters is that she's dead. What matters is not whether that Mexican boy shouted up from the darkness of the deserted street, but the blood in the stairwell. How it got there, after all, was a fact.

Many months from now—months—people will file into the Fox Theater to watch the suspense picture, the one with a motel, that one that looks just like the one out on the west of town, and everyone will see a dark silhouette get up and walk away in a pinched, furious manner.

You will be there and will see only a dark silhouette, but you'll believe those people when they claim it was Dan Watson's mother. She saw what was coming up on-screen. Who—who on earth—ever wants to put themselves in someone else's shoes? To see something so close to them?

The drive-in. The theater. The stairwell. The lawn just past the porch swing. What you do with darkness is pitch yourself into it.

How she reached the stairwell was that the Mexican boy had been downstairs somehow. How it ended there was that Dan Watson had bounded down to the sidewalk. That was a fact. People said there had been a fight out there, that Mexican boy who got deported. But however the fight between the men ended didn't matter. What mattered happened in the stairwell. People said blood had splattered all over the wall. Dan Watson had slammed the green door behind him, shutting away the world. The stairwell had shot into darkness, and that girl had fallen into it, Dan with a fistful of her hair. The two of them pitched backward, her stolen boots slipping, their bodies slamming against the wall. Her back landed with a sharp crack against the edge of a stair. Her head knocked against the wall. She tasted metal in her mouth. She tasted blood.

Did you? Dan Watson asked. Because that is the question everyone wanted to know about that girl. Had she, with that Mexican boy?

Do you take . . . ? the question will come out.

What will be the answer?

That girl bit at his hand, but he only pressed himself harder on top of her. She bit harder and he let go of her hair to slap her once, then a second time, hard enough for her head to hit the wall again. She could not scream because the metallic taste in her mouth had sharpened into a gurgle. Blood had come up from her throat. She sensed it coming, and she would have spit it out in order to cry.

Yes.

When she spat out the blood, the cry came out. They had tumbled all the way down the stairwell, near the street with no one on it at that hour. She opened her eyes, but it was only darkness, only the sweat of Dan's hair, hardly even the light from the top of the stairwell. A pounding came at the green door, closed to the street. Over and over again.

Why was it like that? Didn't the songs make a promise? Didn't the songs say to hold your arms out wide open? Wasn't love supposed to come through an open door to find you?

The dark silhouette stalked out of the theater in disgust, in shame at what she had been forced to see. The quick-witted mother with the pinched face held in her knowledge of two sons—two!—and their suspicious bachelorhoods, the unfairness of it. Everyone with something to keep private.

Her eyes stared up at the darkness of the stairwell, but her heart saw the stars of the theater ceiling, their faint but false twinkle.

Once the song left the soft, beautiful O of Ricky Nelson's mouth, there was only a sweet darkness left behind, not this light. Love was arriving through the open door. She heard its knock, over and over, insistent. A light was coming, brilliant and unstoppable.

Something dark was forming in her throat. A burst of light was forming there. You tried to swallow to keep it from arriving.

You wanted her to close her eyes. You had to force yourself to close them. You know she saw something. You wanted that girl to see something, and there was no going back once she did.

Gracias

MY THANKS TO EVERYONE at Algonquin Books, especially Elisabeth Scharlatt and Chuck Adams, who waited with such patient enthusiasm for this novel. Brunson Hoole and Rachel Careau assisted me tremendously in the final stages of production and I am deeply grateful.

My new colleagues at the University of Arizona have provided me with support and good feeling, as have my students. I especially thank Ted McLoof, Will Pewitt, and Jason Timermanis, who took time from their own work to help me with mine.

This book was started in New York City, and my colleagues at Hachette Book Group remain dedicated supporters: Bob Castillo, Tareth Mitch, David Palmer, Kallie Shimek, and, especially, Harvey-Jane Kowal. Thanks also to my friends who took my absences in stride: Antonio Annunziato, John Antonio, Pierce Mattie, and Aaron Smith.

The New York Foundation for the Arts and the National Endowment for the Arts both provided me with generous support. I cannot express enough gratitude to the Mrs. Giles Whiting Foundation for the inspiration and confidence granted by its tremendous gift in 2008.

Helena María Viramontes, as always, rushed in to assist when I felt most stranded. I aspire to such generosity, as well as to the spirit of support provided by my agent, Stuart Bernstein, a believer all along.